TATTERCOATS

and other Folk Tales

WINIFRED FINLAY

TATTERCOATS

and other Folk Tales

illustrated by Shirley Hughes

HARVEY HOUSE, PUBLISHERS
New York, New York

First published by
Kaye & Ward Ltd
21 New Street, London EC2M 4NT
1976

First published in the United States of America, 1977
by Harvey House, Publishers, 20 Waterside Plaza,
New York, New York, 10010.

5.21

ISBN 0-8178-5532-7

Set in Monophoto Baskerville by
Willmer Brothers Limited, Birkenhead
Printed in Great Britain by
Whitstable Litho Ltd, Whitstable, Kent

Contents

Tattercoats

Long ago there lived a lord whose wife had died shortly after their marriage, leaving him with a daughter whom he loved almost half as much as he loved himself.

When eventually the daughter died, leaving behind her a baby girl, the lord was so unhappy and miserable that he swore he would never look on his granddaughter's face. He gave orders that the child should be put in the care of a nurse and made all the servants swear that his granddaughter should never be allowed anywhere near him.

Then he abandoned himself to his grief.

Sitting by a window which overlooked the cold, grey sea, he wept day and night and night and day and refused to be comforted: the tears coursed down his cheeks and seeped out of the window, to trickle silently away to the ocean, which swallowed them up, caring not a jot for the lord's grief or his selfishness. Longer and longer grew his white hair and beard, creeping gradually over his velvet gown, covering the carved wooden chair on which he sat until the ends buried themselves in the cracks and crevices of the marble floor, which cared as little as did the ocean for the lord's grief or his selfishness.

When the servants in the castle realized that the lord had no love for his granddaughter, they could not think of any reason why they should care for her either, and as she grew up only the nurse looked after her, feeding her on scraps of left-over food, and dressing her in old, torn clothes which no one else would wear.

"Tattercoats!" the servants jeered, pushing her away from the kitchen fire in winter and from the sunny side of the courtyard in summer.

"Tattercoats!" they sneered, aiming blows at her when she shrank from them in the corridors or tried to hide in the dark corners of the dusty, unused rooms.

As she grew older, Tattercoats was driven to seek peace in the countryside or by the seashore, wandering bare-footed all day down lonely lanes or over the ridged sand, finding nuts and berries to stay the pangs of hunger.

Apart from her nurse, she had only one friend – the gooseherd who had come to work for the lord the day she was born. No one knew his name or where he had come from, but as he did not care about any other of the servants, they did not care about him.

As often as she could, Tattercoats stole from the palace in the early morning and waited for the gooseherd to release his clamouring, honking flock and together they drove them to a fresh-water pond in the middle of a green field. Sitting together on a little bank, they watched the geese swim in the pond and then waddle out to feed on the rich grass and wild plants.

"Play a tune for them," Tattercoats begged, as the sun began to sink in the sky.

The gooseherd smiled and softly he played and sweetly, so that the geese thought of nests of grass and leaves and of creamy white eggs from which fluffy goslings would one day emerge, while Tattercoats thought of the blue sky and the waves breaking on the shore and the high song of the planing seabirds, and forgetting how sad and cold and hungry she so often was, she started to dance, her pale golden hair floating round her, and the geese, lifting their heads to the gooseherd's piping, spread their wings and danced around her.

When at last the sun dropped behind the western hills, Tattercoats and the gooseherd returned along the track to the palace, and while the gooseherd slept in a hut by his geese, Tattercoats sought out her nurse to ask if she had found any scraps for her supper, but even when she had to go hungry to bed, the memory of the gooseherd's piping warmed her and filled her with a strange happiness.

Just when it seemed to Tattercoats that she would always have to go hungry and wear ragged clothes, something happened which set the servants in the palace whispering excitedly.

"What is the matter? Why is everyone so excited?" Tattercoats asked her nurse.

"Such wonderful news, my child. At first I would not believe it, but now I find it is true. The king's son has decided to marry but there is no face in all his court which pleases him. Now the prince is travelling with the king throughout the entire land and each of the towns he visits is giving a ball in his honour, so that he can find for himself a girl who is as good as she is lovely, and who is fit to be his bride.

"Tomorrow they visit the town nearest this castle, and you may be sure all the loveliest young ladies will be there – and a great many of the foolish old ones too."

"A ball," Tattercoats breathed. "I have never been to a ball in all my life. How I should love to see all the handsome men and beautiful ladies in their fine clothes. And I wish I could see what the prince looks like."

"So you shall, my pretty one," the nurse said fondly and went straight away to the old lord where he sat in his chair by the window overlooking the grey sea, the tears coursing down his cheeks and trickling silently away to the ocean which carelessly swallowed them up, his long white hair and beard covering his velvet gown while the ends buried themselves in the cracks and crevices of the marble floor.

"Allow my granddaughter to go to the king's ball when I sit here in grief and desolation?" the lord cried angrily when he heard what the nurse had to say. "Never. Go away, woman, and do not mention her existence to me again."

And Tattercoats, who was listening behind the door, sighed sadly.

The very next day, however, a servant entered the chill room, bearing on a silver tray an invitation to the old lord to attend the royal ball.

"Tonight is a night for dancing!" he exclaimed, drying his eyes at once. "Bring me my finest hose and gown and my richest rings and brooches."

The whole castle was in an uproar.

The barber – who had had nothing to do for years – could not be found and it was several hours before the scullion discovered him fishing from the rocks on the seashore. When he saw the state

3

of the old lord's hair and beard, he threw up his hands in dismay, declaring that no instruments he possessed could cut them, whereupon the lord roared for the gardener to bring in his shears, and together gardener and barber cut and hacked and clipped until at last the lord was free of his carved wooden chair.

Meanwhile the other servants were scurrying about, examining the clothes in the wardrobes and chests, beating out the moths, brushing away the dust, arguing as to what could be mended, what washed and ironed, and all agreeing that what was needed was a new suit of clothes altogether but there simply was not time for this to be made.

When at last the lord was shaved and dressed, with a gold chain glittering round his neck, a jewelled clasp adorning the shoulder of his cloak and rings sparkling on his fingers, the nurse approached him again.

"Allow my granddaughter to accompany me to the king's ball when I have sat here for so many years in grief and desolation?" he cried furiously. "Never. Go away, woman, and do not mention her existence to me again or it will be the worse for you."

And Tattercoats, who was listening behind the door, bit her lip to prevent herself from weeping.

Feverishly the servants worked, grooming the horses, repairing and oiling the harness and reins, and cleaning and polishing the carriage so that everything was ready at the exact moment that the old lord descended the palace steps to go to the ball.

It was just as the coachman was helping his master into the coach that the nurse hurried forward and for the third time asked that Tattercoats might be allowed to go to the ball.

"Never!" the old lord shouted angrily. "Go away, woman. If ever you mention my granddaughter's name again, I shall order my servants to turn the pair of you out of the castle and you can both learn to beg for a living."

And Tattercoats, who was listening behind the great oak door, let the tears fall silently from her sad, blue eyes.

"Just imagine – Tattercoats thinking she could go to the ball," the servants jeered, and they pelted her with stale crusts so that she ran sobbing to the field where the gooseherd sat with his flock of geese.

"Why, Tattercoats! I have never seen you crying before. Whatever is the matter?" he asked.

"Tonight is a night for dancing. My grandfather has forgotten his own grief and desolation: he has put on his richest clothes and jewellery and driven off to the ball which the king is giving for his only son. Three times nurse asked him if I could go and three times he refused, telling her never to mention my name again. Oh, dear gooseherd, whatever shall I do?"

"Do, Tattercoats? First you must dry your eyes and then together we shall go to the town and see the king and the prince and the lords and the ladies as they arrive for the ball."

"But I am bare-footed and dressed in rags, dear gooseherd."

"That does not matter to me, nor does it matter to the geese, so come! Let us start at once."

Putting his pipe to his lips the gooseherd played a tune so happy and light-hearted that all sorrow left Tattercoats and smiling with joy, she began to dance.

"Today is indeed a day for dancing, Tattercoats," the gooseherd cried, and hand-in-hand they danced across the field and down the road, and the geese spread out their wings and lifted high their heads and danced after them.

Presently a handsome young man rode up and reined his horse, whereupon the gooseherd stopped piping and Tattercoats and the geese stopped dancing.

"I am sorry to interrupt your revels," the stranger said, "but I have lost my way and wondered if you could tell me where it is that the king is staying tonight?"

"In that town which lies straight ahead," the gooseherd answered, pointing to the distant roofs and spires.

"We are going there ourselves to see him and his son and all the lords and ladies as they arrive for the ball," Tattercoats added happily.

Lifting his pipe to his lips again, the gooseherd played a few soft notes, whereupon the young man jumped off his horse and asked if he might walk there with them.

"Of course," Tattercoats answered, and again the gooseherd played two or three notes of strange, haunting beauty.

"I have never seen such a beautiful girl in all my life," the stranger said, staring at Tattercoats. "Why it is so I can not tell,

5

but this moment I know that I love you more than I ever thought it possible to love any girl. Will you marry me?"

Tattercoats looked at the stranger, smiled a little sadly, and shook her head.

"Why do you make fun of me so?" she asked. "It is not a bare-footed girl dressed in rags that you want for a wife but one of the beautiful ladies, dressed in silks and satins, who will be dancing at the king's ball tonight."

Softly and sweetly the gooseherd played and deeper and deeper the stranger fell in love, but none of his pleas, protests or affirmations had any effect on Tattercoats, who repeated that she was too poor and humble to marry a young man as rich as he.

"If you will not be my wife, then grant me one wish, or life will lose all happiness for me forever," the stranger begged. And still the gooseherd played, softly and enchantingly. "Come to the ball at midnight just as you are now."

"In my torn dress and bare feet?"

"In your torn dress and bare feet and with the gooseherd and the geese as well."

Tattercoats wanted to say that of course she would not go because everyone would laugh at her, but it was the gooseherd who spoke first.

"She will be there," he said, whereupon the young man mounted his horse and rode off to the town.

That night lights blazed from all of the windows in the great castle, and the hall was filled with the sound of music and dancing and of people talking and laughing.

It was one minute to midnight when Tattercoats arrived at the castle door.

"What do you want?" the guard demanded roughly, looking with scorn from Tattercoats to the gooseherd and the flock of geese.

The gooseherd played a few notes, sweeter by far than any heard in the castle that night, and the guard immediately flung open the door.

In stepped Tattercoats, barefooted and wearing her ragged gown, and followed by the gooseherd and his geese. Everyone stopped dancing and moved to the walls, so that a path was cleared through the hall from the door to the far end where the king was sitting, staring, and unable to believe his eyes.

7

Everyone was looking at Tattercoats – everyone except her grandfather who, the moment he saw the ragged gown, had turned away in anger because he had sworn never to look at his granddaughter's face.

As she neared the king, Tattercoats began to tremble with fright, and just as she was about to turn and flee from the ballroom, the stranger whom she had met that day rose from his chair beside the king, and suddenly Tattercoats realized that he was none other than the prince.

Taking her hand in his, the prince kissed her and then turned to his father.

"I have ridden the length and breadth of the kingdom in search of the bride I have known only in my dreams," he said, "and today I found her. Father, this girl, who is as good as she is beautiful, is to be my bride."

The gooseherd raised his pipe to his lips and clear, lovely notes, such as had never been heard there before, filled the hall.

For a moment the place was filled with a dazzling light so that no one could see, and then as the light died away into the soft, yellow flickering of the candles, everyone sighed in awe and amazement, for now Tattercoats stood before them in a white ball gown which sparkled with precious stones. On her head was a golden crown and on her feet she wore golden slippers, while the geese which had danced down the road and followed her into the castle were now changed into little pages dressed in brown doublets and yellow hose.

Of the gooseherd there was no sign and no one ever saw him again, but you may be sure that long after Tattercoats married her prince, she still remembered how kind the gooseherd had been to her and how he had played so softly and sweetly on his magic flute.

As for the old lord, he was more disgruntled than ever to learn that his granddaughter was now a princess and he returned to his palace and sat in his carved wooden chair, staring out at the cold grey sea. His hair grew long again until the ends buried themselves in the cracks and crevices of the marble floor, and tears coursed down his cheeks, seeping out of the window to trickle silently away to the sea which carelessly swallowed them up and cared not a jot for the old man's selfishness.

The Old Handmill

Once upon a time there were two brothers who lived on the east coast of Scotland, by the mouth of a wide river which flowed into the sea.

The younger brother was quite contented to fish offshore and to earn enough to feed and clothe himself and his wife, and because he was kind and polite and as generous as his means would allow, he was well liked both by his neighbours who dwelt on the earth and the Wee Folk who dwelt under it.

The elder brother, however, was selfish and ambitious. He soon gave up fishing for trading and made so much money that he decided he was too important to live down beside the harbour and he built himself a fine house on the top of a neighbouring hill.

One fine summer's day, when the fisherman hauled in his net, he was astonished to find there a magnificent fish, bigger than any he had ever seen before.

Surely this must be the King of all the Fishes, he thought, and rowing back to the harbour, he lifted out his prize triumphantly and set off across the sand to his cottage.

Scarcely had he reached the hillocky ground where the marram grass and sea holly invaded the sand than a Wee Man appeared.

"Good day to ye," the Wee Man said.

"Good day," the fisherman answered politely.

"Surely that must be the King of all the Fishes," the Wee Man commented. "What are ye meaning to do with it?"

"Eat it," the fisherman answered in some surprise.

"Just ye and your wife?" the Wee Man asked.

The fisherman nodded, knowing better than to anger the Wee

9

Man by offering him something he and his kind would in no circumstances eat.

"There's enough there to feed ye and your wife for a couple of weeks," the Wee Man pointed out, "and well ye know that ye'll be lucky to keep it more than a day or two in this hot weather."

"I had not thought of that," the fisherman admitted, for salt was very scarce in those days, and poor people like him could not afford to buy it and so had no way of preserving either meat or fish.

"Offer the fish to your brother who lives in the house on the top of yonder hill," the Wee Man said. "And when he asks what ye want in exchange, tell him ye'll be quite content with the old handmill which stands behind the cellar door."

Thanking the Wee Man for his advice, the fisherman climbed up to the house on the top of the hill.

"Surely this must be the King of the Fishes," the rich brother said. "It is exactly what I want for the feast I am giving tonight. What do ye want for it?"

"Only the old handmill which stands behind the cellar door."

Although the rich brother had never had any use for the old handmill, he was reluctant to part with it when asked for it.

"Why not take a side of bacon?" he suggested, but the fisherman, remembering what the Wee Man had said, shook his head.

"Or a fine hank of wool for your wife to make herself a new shawl?"

The fisherman shook his head again.

"What about a piece of well-dressed leather to make shoes for the coming winter?"

"I'll be quite content with the old handmill which stands behind the cellar door."

Recognizing that the fisherman's mind was quite made up, the elder brother took the King of the Fishes and, with a bad grace, gave the old handmill in exchange.

And what use is this to me, the fisherman wondered, as he made his way downhill and back to his cottage by the seashore.

Scarcely had he reached the hillocky ground where the marram grass and sea holly gave way to the sand than the Wee Man appeared again.

"So ye got the old handmill?" he said.

"Yes. And a hard job I had persuading my brother to part with it, though what use it is neither he nor I know, and what my wife will say when I get home and tell her I have parted with the King of the Fishes for an old handmill, I dare not think."

"Your brother was given it many years ago by mistake and does not know how to use it. But if ye can remember to say 'Grind, mill, grind', your wife will be well content with ye."

"I'll remember that," the fisherman promised and was about to go on when the Wee Man cried,

"Just a minute. There is something else ye must know. Bend down so that I can whisper in your ear."

Obediently the fisherman bent down and the Wee Man whispered a magic word so softly that even the marram grass – which was always whispering secrets to the wind – could not hear it, and then he vanished as suddenly as he had appeared.

Scratching his head, the fisherman looked doubtfully at the old handmill and then returned to his home, putting the mill in the shed where he kept his nets and floats.

That night, when his wife was asleep, he went down to the shed.

"Grind, mill, grind," he ordered. Immediately the mill began to grind out salt and did not stop until at last the fisherman whispered the magic word.

"Husband," the wife exclaimed delightedly the next morning, "how it is so I do not know, but my salt box, which has been empty for months because we are so poor, is now filled to the brim and the salt is spilling over on to the shelf. Ye must go fishing at once because now I can prepare a whole barrel of salt herrings for the winter."

Night after night the fisherman went down to the shed.

"Grind, mill, grind," he ordered, and the mill ground out salt and did not stop until he had whispered the magic word.

"Husband," the wife said at length, "now we have more salt than we can possibly use all year. I shall exchange it for eggs and butter and cheese, and perhaps even sell some in the market place and so make a fine profit."

Each night the old handmill ground away, and gradually word spread that there was always salt to be bought at the fisherman's cottage and people came from far and near and even sailed over the seas from distant lands to buy it, so precious was it.

Now although the fisherman was quite content to go on living as he had always done, his wife grew more and more discontented.

"Why should we live in this tumbledown cottage now?" she demanded. "Why shouldn't we live in a fine house on the top of the hill overlooking the harbour, like your brother and his wife?" And she gave him no peace until at last he built her a fine house like his brother's, but he took care to add a shed at the back where he could store his nets and floats and the old handmill.

Each night he went down to the shed.

"Grind, mill, grind," he ordered, and the mill ground out salt and did not stop until he had whispered the magic word, and each day people came from far and near to buy the precious salt. But it was not long before the wife began to grumble again.

"Now that we are rich, why should I stay at home and do all the housework?" she demanded. "I ought to have a servant lassie to scour the floors and bake the bread and cook the meals."

She gave him no peace until at last he agreed to hire a servant lassie so that his wife could live like a lady. Meanwhile, by night, the handmill ground out salt, and by day, people came from far and near to buy it.

It was not long before the wife began to grumble once more.

"Now that we are rich, why should I stay at home and do nothing?" she demanded. "I want to have new gowns and a carriage and go to feasts and balls and mix with all the fine people."

She gave him no peace until at last he bought her a new gown, hired a carriage and took her to a ball in the neighbouring town where all the fine people were dancing.

They had not long left the house when a sea captain from distant parts came to the door. He had listened to the gossip down at the harbour and knew more about the fisherman's good fortune than he pretended.

When the servant lassie opened the door, he smiled down at her and asked if there was such a thing as an old handmill in the place that she could sell him.

The lassie, not knowing any better and glad to be rid of such a battered old object, fetched the mill from the shed and received in exchange a shining silver coin.

Back to his ship the captain hurried and put out to sea before the fisherman could discover his loss.

The next morning, when they were out of sight of land, the captain put the old handmill on his desk and rubbed his hands with glee.

"Grind, mill, grind," he ordered, and the mill started to grind salt.

"I shall be the wealthiest man in the whole world," the captain cried, as he watched the mound of salt steadily growing until it covered his desk and spilled over on to the floor. "Stop now. That's enough."

But of course the captain did not know the magic word, and so the mill went on grinding and grinding and grinding. Gradually the salt filled the cabin, spilled down into the holds, smothered the crew's quarters and the ship's galley and heaped over the decks until at last the ship sank beneath the weight, down to the bottom of the sea. And there the old handmill lies, still gently grinding and grinding and grinding.

And that is the reason why, to this very day, the sea is salt.

The Five Sisters of Kintail

In the little village of Kintail, which stands at the head of Loch Duich in the Western Highlands of Scotland, there once lived an old farmer with seven beautiful daughters.

There were times when the old man thought it might have been better for him had one of his daughters been a son to help him with the farm work. However, when he looked at the maidens and saw how beautiful they were, he knew that even if it were in his power, he would not change one of the seven for a boy.

There were even times when he thought it might have been better for his peace of mind had all his daughters been sons, because sons obeyed their father and did not unite with sweet smiles and soft voices to coax and persuade and insist so that they always got their own way. However, even when he felt most exasperated and helpless, he only had to look at the maidens and, seeing how beautiful they were, he knew that even if it were in his power, he would not change them for boys.

Some day they will grow up and marry, he told himself, and then I shall have seven strong young men to help me and I shall still have my beautiful daughters to delight me with their graceful movements, their cheerful conversation and their happy laughter.

As time passed, the maidens grew even more attractive, and their father thought with pride that only young men who were rich or of noble blood would be fit suitors for them.

But where, he wondered, could such suitors be found. No one knew better than he how lonely was the countryside where they lived. Few strangers came to Kintail: in those days there were no roads there, and the passes through the mountains were dangerous not only because of the rocks and boulders brought down by the winter's storms, but also because of robbers and desperate men who lived in caves and preyed on unsuspecting travellers.

For some time the old man considered whether perhaps he should leave his farm in the care of a neighbour and undertake the perilous journey to Edinburgh with his daughters. There, he thought, he might find rich and suitable bridegrooms.

Before he had made up his mind, however, winter was upon them with its cold and storms, and he was well content each evening to sit in front of the peat fire with his beautiful daughters and listen to them talking and laughing happily together.

It was just before one midday in January that the sky darkened and a great gale blew out of the north-west, whipping up mountainous seas which crashed on to the rocky coast and flooded into Loch Duich, uprooting trees and tearing the thatched roofs from farms and shielings.

When at last the storm blew itself out, the old man went to see what damage had been done to his land and buildings and was surprised to find a strange ship riding at anchor in the loch, not far from his farm. Her sails were torn to shreds, her mast broken and her timbers so badly damaged that it was obvious that only expert navigation could have brought her through the huge seas of the Atlantic to the relative calm of Loch Duich.

Full of curiosity, he hurried down to the ship and greeted the two young men who appeared on deck, and who were so alike that they were obviously brothers.

"Yours was a fair ship the day you left port, but it seems you must have offended some god of the sea to have put her and yourselves in such peril," he said.

"We know of no god either on sea or land who had cause to wish us such a storm as overtook us yesterday," the elder of the young men answered.

"Indeed, we consulted the Wise Woman before we left our home in Ireland," his brother added, "and she promised us fair weather and good fortune for our entire voyage."

"As the gods have spared our lives," the elder brother continued, "we must now set about making our ship seaworthy again, and that will be no easy matter as we have neither relatives nor friends to help us in your country."

The old man considered the two brothers carefully. They were taller and stronger than any of the men of Kintail and, with their blue eyes and red-gold hair, far more handsome than anyone who dwelt in the farms scattered round the loch: from their manner of speaking, he was convinced they were of noble birth.

"Come home with me and warm yourselves by my fire and while my daughters prepare food for you, let us discuss what must be done to make your ship seaworthy again."

For a few days the brothers – at the earnest entreaty of the seven maidens – rested beside the peat fire in the evenings and strolled with them along the shores of the loch by day, and then finally they pulled their ship ashore.

The old man said that he could provide new timber and the seven daughters said they would be delighted to cut and stitch new sails, and so the brothers started to work, careening and scraping and caulking, measuring and sawing and fitting new timbers.

Never had the maidens been so happy.

There was so much to repair that winter gave way to spring, and spring to summer, and it was not until the first hint of autumn that the work was complete and the ship was ready to sail once more.

Choosing a time when they knew the seven maidens would be out hunting for berries on the slopes of the nearest hill, the two brothers approached the old man and thanked him for all the kindness he had shown them.

"We have one more favour to ask of you," the elder said. "Never in our lives have we seen such beautiful maidens as your daughters. In Ireland we are men of property and high rank. When we marry, our wives will share our fortune and be looked up to by our people."

"You have a mind to marry then?" the old man asked encouragingly.

"Yes. We have both fallen in love – I with your second youngest daughter, my brother with your youngest daughter."

The old man was delighted. Such rich and handsome bridegrooms for two of his daughters! Surely it would not be long before other rich strangers came to Kintail and, seeing his remaining daughters, fell in love with them and married them.

The two youngest maidens were overjoyed when they learned that the brothers had asked for their hands in marriage and rejoiced at the thought that they would sail away over the seas to Ireland, there to live a life of luxury and pleasure.

The other five sisters, however, were so dismayed at the news that for a time they were quite speechless, and then one after the other, they began to weep bitterly and did not cease until their father pointed out that swollen eyes and tear-stained cheeks might ruin their beauty for ever.

"And now what is it that troubles you?" he asked, when at last peace was restored.

"We are seven sisters who have played together and grown up together," the eldest said at length. "As we are all prepared to marry when the right suitors present themselves, we five older ones do not think it either right or proper that the two youngest should be married first.

"We are all equally beautiful. You have often said so yourself. Tell the brothers that it is your opinion that they should choose the two oldest of your daughters."

"Very well," the old man said with a sigh, and avoiding the dismayed looks on the faces of his two youngest daughters, he departed for the ship, where the suitors were awaiting their brides.

Apologetically he explained that while he did indeed welcome them into his family as sons-in-law, life would be much easier for him if they would marry his two eldest daughters.

There was a long and awkward silence.

A frown formed on the face of the younger brother, but before he could speak his mind, the elder put a restraining hand on his arm and then turned to the old man with a courteous smile.

"How can we thank you enough for being so frank with us? To tell you the truth, it was just such a problem that we were discussing when you arrived on board. You see, we are the two youngest of seven sons. Our brothers are taller and stronger and richer than we are."

"And more handsome," the younger brother added eagerly.

"Yes. Much more handsome. Naturally, when we return to Ireland with our brides and tell them of your five beautiful daughters here in Kintail, our five brothers –"

"– who are, of course, not married either –"

"Exactly." The older brother nodded his head. "As I was saying, when we return to Ireland with our brides, our five brothers will immediately set sail –"

"– each in his own ship, and each ship bigger and better equipped than ours."

"Of course." The elder brother nodded his head again. "Our brothers will immediately set sail for Loch Duich and Kintail and ask for permission to marry your five other daughters."

"This being the case," the younger brother concluded, "we must respect the claims of our older brothers and be prepared to accept the hands of your two youngest daughters for ourselves."

After considering the matter, the old man agreed that the young men had made the only possible decision and all three returned to the farm and explained how matters now stood.

The five older sisters, on hearing of the five rich and handsome suitors in Ireland, brightened up immediately and withdrew all objections to the marriage. The ceremony was celebrated at once and the two brothers and their brides sailed away out of Loch Duich, past Skye and the other islands of the Hebrides, and back to their home in Ireland.

As for the five remaining sisters, they went down daily to the shores of the loch and watched and waited, growing – so it seemed to their father – more beautiful each day as they dreamed of the handsome lovers who would come sailing over the seas to claim them.

Naturally people talked of the beauty of the five sisters, and men travelled from far and near, fell in love at first sight, and begged to be allowed to marry first one and then another of the maidens, but although their father was willing enough, his daughters proved quite impossible to please.

One suitor was too small and another too tall: this one was too thin and that too fat: the fifth was a spendthrift and the sixth a miser, and not one of them had any pretensions at all to good looks.

"We know the kind of husbands we want," the maidens said

firmly, "and we are quite willing to wait until they come to claim us." And they returned to their dreams of tall, handsome young men – but not too young, of course – with blue eyes and red-gold hair, who would come sailing over the seas to claim them.

Slowly the years slipped by and the old man, knowing that he had to make some kind of provision for his five daughters before death claimed him, set off one day with gifts of milk and eggs and game to consult the Wise Man of the Corries.

"Let me see my daughters' suitors for myself in the Pool of Knowledge," he begged, "and then my mind can know some peace."

"Think what you ask," the Wise Man answered. "I can make the pool reveal the future, but what you see may not bring you the peace of mind you seek."

"I must see for myself," the old man insisted, and so the Wise Man led him through a cleft in the hills to a dark peat pool, its banks fringed with rushes and yellow flags and forget-me-nots. Standing on a boulder at the edge of the pool, the Wise Man uttered his charms in a high, keening cry and then bade the old man climb on the rock beside him, look into the water, and see what was mirrored there.

Minute after minute the old man stared into the placid pool and then finally he shook his head.

"I see nothing at all," he confessed sadly. "I know now what I have long thought – there are no young men such as the two brothers described."

"Go back and tell your five daughters the suitors they wait for are only dreams," the Wise Man advised. "Tell them they would be well advised to marry the farmers and fishermen who have offered for them."

"Marry a farmer!" the eldest cried indignantly.

"Or a fisherman!" the second said scornfully.

"Have you forgotten that our two youngest sisters are living in luxury in Ireland?" the third asked.

"And by this time are probably queens," the fourth added.

"We know the kind of husbands we want," the fifth said softly, "and we are all agreed that we shall watch and wait until they come to claim us."

And they returned once more to their dreams of tall handsome

young men with blue eyes and red-gold hair, who would come sailing over the seas to claim them.

More years passed and the old man, knowing that his end was near, sent, late one night, for the Wise Man of the Corries, and long and earnestly they talked while the five sisters slept and dreamed their dreams.

The next morning, when they awoke, they found that their father was dead and the Wise Man was sitting in his chair.

"Last night I talked long with your father," he said, "and I gave him my word that I would do the best I could when there was no one here to care for you.

"Now that this time has come, you will do well to listen to the advice I gave your father when he visited me and looked long into the Pool of Knowledge in the corrie. Marry immediately, choosing husbands from the farmers and fishermen who have already offered for you. They will look after you and see that you come to no harm."

"Never!" The five sisters shook their heads proudly. "Ever since our two youngest sisters left us, we have watched and waited together for our bridegroom to come sailing over the seas to claim us, and we shall continue to watch and wait."

"Even though your father saw in the Pool of Knowledge that your suitors were only dreams?"

But nothing the Wise Man said could make the sisters change their minds. For many years they had waited and watched together, and they would go on waiting and watching for ever.

"All your lives you have had your own way," the Wise Man said with a sigh, "and I promised your father I would not go against your wishes when he died.

"You have refused to listen to both his advice and mine. Now you shall do exactly as you yourselves have chosen. You shall remain here forever together at Kintail, forever watching and forever waiting, but to protect you from the miseries and unhappiness of this life I shall turn you into five mountains, so beautiful that artists will paint pictures of you and poets write poems about you and you will gladden the eyes of all who see you."

And that is why to this day, if you journey through the Western Highlands of Scotland to Kyle of Lochalsh and the island of Skye, you will see the mountains – which are still called the Five Sisters of Kintail – standing at the head of Loch Duich, and if you have time to stop and gaze at them, you will see how beautiful they are as they watch and wait, gazing over the waters of the loch and past the Cuillins of Skye, waiting for the ships that never come, for the suitors with blue eyes and red-gold hair who were only dreams.

The Earl of Mar's Daughter

Long ago there lived in Scotland a rich and powerful nobleman, the Earl of Mar, who had one fair daughter.

As the Earl wanted a rich bridegroom for his daughter, and as the girl wanted a husband she could love all her life, both were content to wait for the right suitor.

Now one day, when the Earl's daughter was sitting beneath a green tree in her garden, she saw a dove perched on the tower above, looking down at her and cooing softly. He was such a handsome bird and he looked at her so longingly that she knew she did not want him to fly away.

"Coo-my-doo," she called gently. "Come down and live with me. I will give you a red-gold cage lined with silver, and feed you and care for you as no one else has ever done."

Immediately the dove flew down to her, and she took him to her room and gave orders that a red-gold cage was to be fashioned before nightfall, and because she was the Earl of Mar's daughter, the cage was ready one minute before the setting of the sun.

"Sleep well, Coo-my-doo," she whispered that night before falling fast asleep. At midnight she awoke to find the moonlight streaming through her window on to a handsome young man who knelt beside her bed.

"Who are you and how did you get here?" she asked in alarm.

"Do not be frightened," the young man said. "I am Coo-my-doo, the bird you brought to your room today. My mother is a queen and an enchantress in a far-off land. When I told her that I wanted to roam the world in search of a wife I could love for ever, she cast a spell to help me. I am a dove by day and a man by

night. Long have I searched for the girl I could love and today I have found her. All I want now is to live with you until the day I die."

"And I love you, Coo-my-doo," the Earl's daughter replied. "I will be your wife and live with you until the day I die."

Hand in hand they stole through the sleeping castle and out of the garden by a secret door to which only the Earl's daughter had a key. Through a dark wood they hurried to an old hermit who had known and loved the girl since she was a child, and, with the birds and animals that hunted by night as witnesses, he married the young people and then, just as silently as they had come, they returned to the castle.

For a whole year they lived together in great happiness, and then the Earl of Mar's daughter gave birth to a fine son. Immediately Coo-my-doo carried the boy off to the Queen, his mother, to be cared for and brought up as befitted one of royal blood.

Each year afterwards, for six more years, a son was born, and each time was carried off to the Queen, to be cared for and brought up as befitted one of royal blood.

For three and twenty years Coo-my-doo and the Earl of Mar's daughter lived happily together until one day a very wealthy nobleman came to ask the Earl for his daughter's hand in marriage. She, however, refused to see the suitor and sent back all his presents.

"I am quite content to live alone with Coo-my-doo," she told her father.

At this, the Earl lost his temper.

"This morning, before I eat or drink, I shall kill that bird," he swore, "and tomorrow you shall marry this nobleman."

When Coo-my-doo heard this, he waited no longer but flew straight back to the Queen, his mother.

"Welcome home, Prince Florentine," the Queen cried. "Tonight I shall hold a ball in honour of your return home."

"Now is no time for a ball, Lady Mother. Now I must have your help, or the wife I love so dearly will be forced to marry another."

"What help is it you want, my son, Florentine?"

"Turn four and twenty of your men at arms into grey storks,

and turn my seven sons into seven swans and turn me into a gay goshawk, a bird of high degree."

With the help of a Wise Woman, who was even more versed in magic than she was, the Queen did as her son asked, and over the sea flew the four and twenty grey storks, the seven swans and the gay goshawk, the bird of high degree.

Down into the garden they flew just as the guests had assembled for the wedding. The grey storks seized the men-at-arms so that they could neither fight nor run away; the swans bound the bridegroom to a tree so that he could move neither hand nor foot, and then the birds closed round the Earl of Mar's daughter and bore her up and away, with the wedding guests staring open-mouthed, unable to believe their eyes.

When the Earl of Mar learned how long his daughter and the Prince Florentine had loved each other and how they had seven brave sons, then of course he forgave them at once and was made welcome whenever he sailed over the seas to visit them.

So it was that the Earl of Mar's daughter, with the Prince Florentine – who she always called Coo-my-doo – and their seven handsome sons lived happily ever after.

Note. "Doo" is the Scottish word for "dove"

The Three Feathers

A long, long time ago, in the far north of Scotland, there lived a king who had three sons. The king made no secret of the fact that he preferred the company of the two older princes, who had a very good opinion of themselves, were given to horseplay and crude practical jokes and despised their young brother.

"The lad was born a fool," the king used to say scornfully. "He is growing up to be bigger fool, and before he is of age he will be the biggest fool in all my kingdom." And while everyone – except the chamberlain – laughed, the youngest son thought a great deal but said nothing.

Now as the years passed, the king fell ill, and when the day came that he could not rise from his couch, he decided that he would have to choose who should reign after him.

"Both my elder sons are handsome, brave and resourceful," he said to his chamberlain. "How am I to decide between them?"

"Send them out into the world for a year and a day," the chamberlain answered. For years the two elder princes had amused themselves by putting beetles and slowworms in his bed and tripping him up so that he fell in the castle pond, and he had been waiting for the chance to have some peace. "Tell them that the one who brings back the finest and most beautiful ring will be your heir and reign here after you. And you might as well send the youngest prince too," he added, turning away so that the king should not see the thoughtful look in his eyes.

"But in which direction should we go to look for the rings?" the two elder princes asked, when the king told them what he had in mind for them.

The king turned to the chamberlain.

"Leave that to me, sire," the old man answered. He had planned it all the very day the two princes had goaded his horse with a chestnut burr so that it bolted, tossing him head first through a briar bush and into a bed of stinging nettles: everyone had laughed except the youngest prince, who had helped him to his feet and then applied dock leaves to the painful stings.

"Come with me," he said, and the three princes and all the courtiers followed him up the stone stairs, and round and round and round until at length they reached the battlements of the castle. Here he gave each of the princes a white feather, tipped with dark brown, from the tail of the golden eaglet which nested in the rocky summit of the highest mountain in the kingdom.

"Throw your feathers into the air," he ordered, "and let the winds decide in which direction you should go."

Immediately the eldest prince threw his feather in the air, and the North Wind seized it and bore it away; then the second prince threw his feather and watched as the South Wind carried it off; but when the youngest prince held out his feather, there was not a breath of wind anywhere, and idly twisting and twirling, it dropped down the castle wall and was lost in a patch of thistles which grew in the courtyard below.

"He was born a fool," the eldest prince cried. "He's growing up to be a bigger fool, and before he comes of age he will be the biggest fool in all the kingdom."

"No journeying and exciting adventures for you," the second prince mocked. "You stay here and work in the kitchen."

"And make sure you have a fine meal ready for us when we return in a year and a day," the eldest added.

They both hurried down the winding stone stairs, round and round and round, and out into the courtyard, where the eldest mounted his black horse and set off to the north in search of his ring, and the second mounted his brown horse and galloped away to the south.

As for the youngest prince, he sighed, and spent his days wandering on foot over the moors, or sitting on the banks of the burn which ran between the heather, bracken and yellow whin. He watched the hawk which circled overhead, the moorhen which jerked its tail as it swam and the deer that came down, velvet-footed, to slake its thirst, and so interested was he in all that went on around him that he paid little attention to the old, wrinkled frog which stared at him so often from the opposite bank and croaked so harshly.

As the days became weeks, and the weeks months, it seemed to the young prince that the hawk with its mewing cry, the moorhen with its clucking and the deer with its bellowing, were talking to him in their own language, and he hoped that the day might soon come when he would be able to understand just what they were saying.

When eleven months and one day of the year had passed, the chamberlain waylaid him as he was going out of the kitchen door.

"I wonder what happened to that eaglet's feather which twisted and twirled from the battlements," he said.

The young prince halted. He had forgotten all about the feather and the search for a ring, but now he decided that perhaps he ought to give the matter some thought. Going out into the courtyard, he parted the thistles – which had grown twice as high and prickly as the previous year – and before long found his feather lying on top of an iron ring let into a heavy flagstone.

"I never knew that ring was there before," he said, turning to the chamberlain. "I wonder what it is for."

"Pull it up and see," the chamberlain suggested.

Grasping the iron ring, the prince pulled with all his might and lifted up the flagstone. To his amazement he saw a flight of stone steps disappearing into the darkness underneath the castle.

"I never knew those steps were there before," he said. "I wonder where they lead to."

"Climb down and see," the chamberlain replied, and disappeared into the castle.

Down the steps the prince climbed until at last he reached the bottom.

"It has taken you long enough to get here," a harsh voice cried impatiently. "I was just beginning to wonder if your father was right after all, and if you really were a fool."

Surprised, the prince looked around him, and at length his eyes dropped to the floor where he saw an old, wrinkled frog staring up at him.

"Was it you who sat on the opposite bank and croaked so often?" he asked.

"It was. I nearly made myself hoarse, inviting you to the Kingdom of the Frogs, but would you listen? Dear me! No!"

"I am very sorry," the prince said humbly. "The trouble was that I did not understand your language then."

"Oh." The frog looked mollified. "In that case you had better follow me."

He led the prince into a splendid hall hung with silken spiders' webs adorned with dewdrops and lit by a thousand glowworms. On either side of a long banqueting table laden with the most delicious food, sat a number of frogs who clapped excitedly when the prince entered.

"You are to sit at the top of the table," the old frog said, as the clapping died away. "You are our guest of honour because never in your life have you harmed any of our number."

For a whole month the prince stayed in the Kingdom of the Frogs, feasting and laughing, talking and dancing: never had he been so happy, and probably he would have been quite contented to stay there for the rest of his life had not the old frog drawn him to one side.

"Today the year and a day are over," he said. "Your elder brothers returned to the castle this morning and you must go back tonight. Here is the finest ring in the Kingdom of the Frogs. Take it with the same happiness that we give it to you, and for the time being forget that you ever understood our language."

The prince took the ring, knowing it was the finest he had ever seen in his life and, thanking the frogs for their kindness, he climbed up the stone steps to the courtyard and went into the castle where his father lay sick upon his couch, and his two elder brothers were arguing as to who had brought back the finer ring.

When they saw the youngest brother's ring, the king, the princes and the courtiers all fell silent, staring at the emeralds which gleamed and glittered in the rushlight.

"There is no doubt about it, sire," the chamberlain said. "Your youngest son has brought you the finest and most beautiful ring in the kingdom."

"It is worth more than the other two rings put together," one of the courtiers remarked.

"That means that the youngest prince will be the heir to his father's kingdom," another added.

The two elder princes were extremely angry. Turning to the king, they pointed out that for a whole year and a day they had journeyed far, one to the north, the other to the south, undergoing all kinds of perilous adventures, risking their lives in the search for a ring to please their father, while their young brother had stayed safely at home in the castle, and by sheer good luck had found his ring lying in the courtyard.

"Let us have another chance," they cried. "We can prove how superior we are to that foolish brother of ours."

"Both my elder sons are handsome, brave and resourceful," the king said to his chamberlain. "What other test can we devise so that they can prove this and I can choose between them?"

"Send them away once again for a year and a day," the chamberlain answered. "Let them follow their feathers as before, and the one who brings back the most beautiful princess, to wear the most beautiful ring, shall be your heir and reign after you."

Up to the battlements climbed the chamberlain, the princes and the courtiers, round and round and round. Once again the young men were each given a white feather tipped with dark brown, but this time there was less white and more brown, for the bird on the rocky summit was now a full grown eagle.

As the eldest prince threw his feather in the air, the East Wind seized it and bore it away, and when the second prince threw up his feather, the West Wind carried it off. But there was not a breath of wind as the youngest prince let fall his feather, so that idly turning and twisting it dropped down the castle wall and was lost in the patch of thistles which grew in the courtyard below.

"He was born a fool," the eldest prince cried. "He is growing up to be a bigger fool, and before he comes of age he will be the biggest fool in all the kingdom."

"No journeying and exciting adventures for you," the second prince mocked. "You stay here and work in the kitchen."

"And make sure you have a fine meal ready for us when we return in a year and a day," the eldest added.

They both hurried down the winding stone stairs, round and round and round, and out into the courtyard, where the eldest mounted his black horse and set off to the east in search of his princess, and the second galloped away to the west on his brown horse.

As for the youngest prince, he sighed, and spent his days as he had the previous year, wandering over the moors or sitting on the banks of the burn by the nodding harebells, and though he watched the hawk, the moorhen and the deer, he paid little attention to the old, wrinkled frog which stared at him so often from the opposite bank and croaked so harshly.

When eleven months and one day of the year had passed, the chamberlain waylaid him as he was going out of the kitchen door.

"I wonder what happened to that eagle's feather which twisted and twirled from the battlements," he said.

The young prince halted. He had forgotten all about the feather and the search for a princess, but now he decided that perhaps he ought to give the matter some thought. Going out into the courtyard, he parted the thistles – which had grown even higher and more prickly – and found his feather on the iron ring. A few minutes later he was climbing down the stone steps again, and there was the old frog, waiting for him in exactly the same place as before.

"Only four weeks," the old frog muttered, leading the prince along to the banqueting hall. "We have not got very much time to find you a princess, have we? Now take your place at the top of the table and enjoy yourself in the Kingdom of the Frogs."

The young prince did as he was bid, and just as the feast was over a little green frog jumped on to his knee and looked at him as though trying to tell him something very important.

"Poor wee froggie," the prince said, stroking it tenderly. "Bonnie wee froggie. What is it you want then?" But the frog only gazed into his eyes and never a word did it utter.

Each evening the frog jumped on to the prince's knee and looked into his eyes: each time he stroked it and asked what it wanted, but never a word did it utter.

At last the month passed and the old frog drew him to one side.

"Time is getting short," he said. "Your elder brothers returned to the castle this morning and you must go back tonight and take with you the most beautiful princess in the kingdom." And he pointed to the little green frog.

The prince could not believe either his ears or his eyes.

"My father and my brothers have been calling me a fool all my life," he said. "If I go back and tell them this wee froggie is a princess, they will know they have been right, and so will everyone in the kingdom." And he turned away so that he should not see the sorrow in the eyes of the little green frog.

"We found you the most beautiful ring in the world," the old frog reminded him. "Trust us and we shall find you the most beautiful princess."

"You are the only people who have been kind to me – except the chamberlain," the prince answered at length. "Very well. I shall trust you."

"Good," cried the old frog, and immediately gave orders for a splendid wedding with bells ringing and trumpets sounding, and amidst great rejoicing the prince married the little green frog.

"Now you must go back to the castle," the old frog said. "You will find your bride waiting for you in the courtyard."

With a sinking heart the prince climbed up the stone steps. And stared.

There stood a splendid carriage of gold drawn by six white horses and attended by footmen in livery, soldiers in uniform and a crowd of laughing, cheering courtiers.

But that was not all.

Inside the coach sat the most beautiful princess the prince had ever seen in his life or dreamed of in his dreams.

"Are you my wee green froggie?" he asked.

"I am," the princess answered. "And all these are my people. Because you trusted us and married me, you broke the spell which turned us into frogs."

Joyfully the prince helped the beautiful princess out of her carriage of gold, and hand in hand they walked into the castle where the king lay sick upon his couch and the two elder brothers were arguing as to who had brought back the most beautiful princess.

The moment the king saw his youngest son's bride he sat up for the first time for two years.

"My youngest son has brought home the most beautiful princess in all the kingdom," he cried. "Chamberlain, bring the most beautiful ring in the land that my son may place it on the

35

finger of his bride. Perhaps he is not quite such a fool as I thought."

"He has never been a fool at all, sire," the chamberlain remarked, and the youngest prince wondered for a fleeting moment why the old man reminded him so strongly of the wrinkled old frog.

"I am completely cured," the king cried jumping off his couch. "We shall have a splendid banquet lasting seven days and seven nights. After that my two elder sons must ride off with their princesses and find castles and lands of their own, for I can see there will be no place for them here.

"As for you" – and he turned to his youngest son – "I always knew you were the most handsome, brave and resourceful of them all. You and your bride shall reign here after me."

"Why not let them start now?" the chamberlain suggested. "You would then be free to feast and hunt and fish to your heart's content."

That is exactly what happened, and the youngest prince and the beautiful princess, the king and the chamberlain, lived together happily for a long, long time and are remembered to this very day.

Nicht Nought Nothing

Once upon a time, and a long time ago it was, there lived a king and queen whose dearest wish was to have a son whom they could love and cherish and who would inherit the kingdom after them.

At length, just when they had almost given up hope, the queen gave birth to a fine bairn. As the king was journeying in far-off lands at the time, the queen announced that there would be no christening until he returned and chose a name for his heir.

"In the meantime we shall call him" – the queen paused and thought for a moment – "Of course! We shall call him Nicht Nought Nothing."

"Nicht Nought Nothing," the courtiers repeated. "Yes, that is a splendid name to be going on with." And Nicht Nought Nothing the bairn was called by queen and courtiers and servants alike.

Now what with battles and feasts and various adventures with dragons and sea monsters, the king was away much longer than anyone expected and knew nothing of the son who had been born and had grown into a fine bairn, the very image of his father.

At length, however, wearying of travel in strange lands, the king decided to return to his own kingdom. He had covered more than half the distance back when he found his way barred by a fast-flowing river, too wide and too deep for him to cross and never a bridge in sight.

As he was wondering what to do, a giant approached him.

"It would be no trouble for me to carry you across yon river," he said.

"What do you want in payment?" the king demanded.

"All I want is Nicht Nought Nothing," the giant answered.

"What a fine, generous fellow you are," the king said happily, and climbed on the giant's back. "Now are you sure I can't give you anything for your trouble?" he inquired, as the giant set him down safe and dry on the far bank.

"All I want is Nicht Nought Nothing," the giant repeated, and strode off without another word.

When the king finally arrived home, he was delighted to find he had a handsome young son who was the very image of himself.

"I waited for you to return so that you could choose a name for him," the queen said. "Until this day we have all called him Nicht Nought Nothing."

On hearing this, the king grew pale and sank, trembling, on to a couch.

"What have I done?" he cried. "A giant in a faraway land carried me over a river which was too wide and too deep for me to cross, and never a bridge in sight. When I asked him what I should give him in payment, he said that all he wanted was Nicht Nought Nothing. How was I to know that at that time I had a son and his name was Nicht Nought Nothing?"

"You should have known better than to trust giants and creatures like that," the queen said angrily. "He tricked you. To save our bairn, now we must trick him. When he comes here, as he must surely do, we will give him the hen-wife's bairn."

The very next day the giant came striding up to the palace.

"Do you remember me?" he asked the king.

"I do," the king answered. "You carried me over a river which was too wide and too deep for me to cross, and never a bridge in sight."

"And do you remember what I asked in return?" the giant demanded.

"I do," the king answered with a sigh. "You said all that you wanted was Nicht Nought Nothing."

"You gave your word. Now keep it."

"Certainly," the king replied, and sent for the hen-wife's bairn who had been washed and scrubbed and dressed in princely clothes, and the giant set him on his shoulder and left the palace without another word.

Over hill and moorland, through bracken and heather, the

giant strode, until he came to a large boulder in the middle of a green field, and there he sat down.

"Hidge, Hodge on my back, what time of day is it?" he asked suddenly.

"Time of day? Why, at this very moment my mother, the henwife, will be picking out the biggest and brownest of the new-laid eggs to take up to the royal palace," the bairn answered, knowing no better than to tell the truth.

"I have been tricked!" the giant roared, and plucking the bairn from his shoulder, he threw him down on the grass. "Find your own way home, wretch."

Back to the palace he hurried, where the king and queen said their servants must have made a mistake, and this time they gave him the gardener's bairn who had been washed and scrubbed and dressed in princely clothes. Picking him up, the giant set him on his shoulder and left the palace without another word.

Over hill and moorland, through bracken and heather, he strode, the bairn on his shoulder, until at length he came to the large boulder in the middle of the green field, and there he sat down again.

"Hidge, Hodge on my back, what time of day is it?" he asked suddenly.

"Time of day? Why, at this very moment my father, the gardener, will be digging up turnips for the king's dinner," the bairn answered, knowing no better than to tell the truth.

"I have been tricked again!" the giant roared, and plucking the bairn from his shoulder, he threw him down on the grass. "Find your own way home, wretch."

Back to the palace he hurried, his face red, his eyes glaring.

"Twice you have tried to trick me and twice you have failed!" he shouted in a terrible voice. "Give me Nicht Nought Nothing or I will bring down the palace about your heads and destroy you and every living soul in it."

Knowing that now there was nothing more they could do, the king and queen produced their own bairn and the giant picked him up and set him on his shoulder and then strode off over hill and moorland, through bracken and heather, until he came to the boulder in the middle of the green field, and there he sat down once more.

"Hidge, Hodge on my back, what time of day is it?" he asked suddenly.

"It is the time the king, my father, and the queen, my mother will be sitting down to eat, and they will both be weeping because I am not with them," the bairn answered, and the giant nodded his head, satisfied that at last he had been given Nicht Nought Nothing.

"Now we shall return to my house," he said, setting off again. "I already have one bonnie daughter and today I have got myself a bonnie son. If you behave yourself and don't try to be too clever I dare say we shall all get on very nicely."

The giant's daughter was very pleased when her father brought her a playmate and liked Nicht Nought Nothing as well as he liked her. The two bairns played together with never a cross word, and as Nicht Nought Nothing behaved himself and didn't try to be too clever, the giant was well satisfied.

As the years passed, however, the bairns grew up and became fonder of each other than the giant cared for, so that at last he decided that there was nothing for it but to rid himself of Nicht Nought Nothing.

"You have idled away all these years in my house," he stormed one evening. "Tomorrow you can do some work for a change. At the bottom of the paddock is a stable seven miles long and seven miles broad which has not been cleaned for seven years. See it is clean by nightfall tomorrow or I will have you for my supper."

The next day Nicht Nought Nothing was up and at work in the stable before daybreak, but when the giant's daughter brought him his dinner, he was in despair.

"Seven hours have I laboured here, but the faster I clean out the dirt, the more it seems to increase."

"Come into the paddock and eat your dinner and rest a while," the giant's daughter said, "and perhaps I can think of some way to help you."

Nicht Nought Nothing left the stable, ate his dinner and, exhausted by his hard work, stretched out in the sunshine on the green grass and fell fast asleep.

As soon as she saw this, the giant's daughter got to her feet and held out her arms.

"Come to me, all you beasts in the field and all you birds in the air," she cried. "Come and help Nicht Nought Nothing clean out my father's stable."

In the twinkling of an eye all the beasts in the field and the birds in the air carried off the dirt of seven years, so that when Nicht Nought Nothing woke up the stable was as clean as the day it had been built, and knowing that the giant's daughter had done this for him, he loved her dearly.

When the giant came home in the evening and saw what had happened his face grew red with anger.

"It will fare ill with the one who helped you when I find out who it was," he cried. "But don't think you can escape me. On the far side of that hill there is a loch seven miles long and seven miles wide and seven miles deep. Empty it tomorrow or I will have you for my supper."

The next day Nicht Nought Nothing was up and at work by the lochside before daybreak, but when the giant's daughter brought him his dinner, he was in despair again.

"Seven hours have I laboured here, but no matter how much water I carry away in my pail, the level of the loch doesn't fall a fraction of an inch."

"Come over to this bank of wild thyme and eat your dinner and rest a while," the giant's daughter said, "and perhaps I can think of some way to help you."

Nicht Nought Nothing left the loch, ate his dinner and, exhausted by his hard work, stretched out in the sunshine on the bank of wild thyme and fell fast asleep.

As soon as she saw this, the giant's daughter got to her feet and held out her arms.

"Come to me, all you fish of the sea, whether you be great or whether you be small, and drink the loch dry to help Nicht Nought Nothing."

In the twinkling of an eye the fish in the sea, small and great, had drained dry the loch, so that when Nicht Nought Nothing woke up there was but one drop of water glinting in a curved stone on the dry bed of the loch, and knowing that the giant's daughter had done this for him, he loved her exceedingly.

When the giant came home in the evening and saw what had happened his face grew red with anger and he seized a poker from the hearth and bent it in two with the grip of his hands.

"It will fare ill with the one who helped you when I find out who it was," he cried. "But don't think you can escape me. On the far side of yonder wood there is a tree seven miles high, with never a branch on it except at the very top and there a bird has built its nest and laid its eggs. Bring down those eggs without so much as chipping the shell of one of them or I will have you for my supper."

The next day the giant's daughter rose when Nicht Nought Nothing got up and together they went to the tree that was seven miles high, with never a branch on it except at the very top and there a bird had built its nest.

"This is difficult but not impossible," the giant's daughter said. "Sit down while I think, but whatever happens, don't fall asleep."

Nicht Nought Nothing sat down and watched as she summoned up all her magic until at last she had made steps of her fingers and toes and he was able to climb to the nest at the top of the tree. Carefully he lifted out the eggs and climbed down again, but just as he reached the ground he dropped one of the eggs and it broke.

"There is no hope for us now," the giant's daughter said. "You must fly from here at once, and as my father will know I have helped you, you must take me with you."

Hand in hand they ran off through bracken and heather and over hills and moorland.

"I hear a sound behind us that fills me with fear," Nicht Nought Nothing said, stopping for a moment to listen.

"It is only the wind in the pine trees," the giant's daughter answered, and on they ran.

"I hear a sound behind us that is louder now and fills me with terror," Nicht Nought Nothing said, stopping to listen.

"It is only the flighting of the wild white swans," the giant's daughter answered, and on they ran.

"I hear a sound close behind us and now I know it to be the voice of the giant who hates us both and will kill us," Nicht Nought Nothing said, stopping again to listen.

"Run on, run on and never look back," the giant's daughter urged. "When you reach your father's palace, wait there for me.

But remember this one thing. Until I come to you, let no one kiss you on the mouth and then all will be well between us."

On Nicht Nought Nothing ran, but the giant's daughter – who was no more the giant's daughter than Nicht Nought Nothing his son – thought harder than she had ever thought before. Just as the giant appeared on the brow of a hill she summoned up all her magic and a deep lochan suddenly separated them. So angry was the giant that he took no account of where he was going and he fell into the lochan and was drowned.

And that was the end of him.

When Nicht Nought Nothing reached the palace gates, one of the hounds, recognizing him for what he was, jumped up joyfully and licked his lips, so that immediately he forgot all about the giant and the young lady who had saved his life.

It was so long since they had lost their son that neither the king nor the queen recognized Nicht Nought Nothing. As was their custom, however, they welcomed him and treated him kindly, but they could not help wondering why he slept so much and why, when he was awake, he sighed so often and spoke so little.

"We must find him a fine lady for a wife," they said, "and then he will be happy and contented." And they sent out messengers to the four corners of the kingdom, announcing that a rich dowry would be given to a bride suitable for the young stranger.

When the giant's daughter arrived at the palace she slipped into the garden and climbed up into an apple tree growing by a pond, there to wait until Nicht Nought Nothing came out to claim her.

As she sat among the green leaves, the gardener's daughter, passing underneath, saw in the pond the reflection of the face of the young lady in the tree.

"How beautiful I am," she cried, peering into the water. "I shall tell my father I am much too beautiful to work in the garden. This very day I'll go to the king and queen and tell them I'm the bride they are seeking for the handsome stranger who sleeps so much and sighs and speaks so little when he is awake."

A little later the gardener's wife passed under the tree and saw in the pond the reflection of the face of the young lady in the tree.

"How beautiful I am," she cried. "I shall tell my husband I am too beautiful to be married to him. This very day I shall go to the king and queen and tell them I'm the bride they are seeking for the handsome stranger who sleeps so much and speaks so little when he is awake."

When the gardener heard what both his daughter and his wife had to say he went to the apple tree by the pond, and looking up, he saw the bonny young lady sitting amongst the green leaves.

"Who are you and what are you looking for?" he asked.

"I am a young lady from a far-off land and I have come to marry the stranger who arrived at the palace a few days ago."

"Then you are too late, bonny young lady. The king and the queen have already chosen a bride and the marriage is to be celebrated this very day."

"If you'll take me to him, I promise you'll have no cause to rue it."

"Give me your hand, young lady," the gardener said, and he helped her down from the apple tree and led her into the palace, where there was a great deal of hurrying about and excitement because of the wedding. The only one who took no part in the proceedings was the bridegroom himself, and he slept in a chair, his face sad and pale.

The moment she saw the sleeping stranger, the young lady flung herself down on her knees beside him.

"I have come to you as I said I would," she cried. "Waken and speak to me."

But the young man only sighed and slept on, and the young lady knew he must have forgotten what she told him and allowed someone to kiss his lips.

"I cleared the stable, I laved the loch, and I clomb the tree,
And all for love of thee,
And thou wilt not waken and speak to me,"
   she cried desperately.

When the king and queen heard this, they asked the bonny young lady what she meant, as the young man said nothing of a stable, a loch, or a tree.

"Three times I saved the life of Nicht Nought Nothing," the young lady said, "and now he will not waken and speak to me."

"Nicht Nought Nothing!" the king cried in astonishment.

"You mean this stranger sleeping in the chair is our bairn?" the queen asked.

"If Nicht Nought Nothing is your bairn, then this indeed is your son and my true love," the young lady answered, whereupon the king and the queen too knelt down by the young man and embraced him and wept and called him their son and begged him to waken and speak to them.

And Nicht Nought Nothing yawned. And stretched his arms. And woke up.

When he saw the bonny young lady he recognized her at once for his own true love and told the king and the queen all she had done for him and how much he loved her.

Of course the king and the queen were overjoyed to have their son back safe and sound, and Nicht Nought Nothing and the bonny young lady were married that very day, and they all lived happily ever after.

The Bird with the Gift of Fire

In the very beginning of time – so the mothers of Islay, in the Hebrides, used to tell their children – and before fire was known on earth, all the birds lived on Tir-nan-Og and only visited the world occasionally.

Tir-nan-Og, the Land of Youth, lay far over the sea to the west of the Hebrides. Here the grass was always green and the lochans were gay with waterlilies and fringed with bog cotton and forget-me-nots: ripe fruit hung on the trees all the year round, and overhead the sun shone in a blue sky by day and the moon gleamed silver and bright by night.

To this island came not only the heroes who had fought and died valiantly on earth, but also ordinary men and women who had lived quiet and humble lives, and no matter how old or sick they might have been, the moment they set foot on Tir-nan-Og they became young and handsome and agile. In the daytime they strolled through the green grass or rode or hunted, and when night fell they gathered round the fires in the great halls – fires which never needed to be replenished with wood or peat and which burned with flames of red and gold and green – and there they feasted and listened to tales of the heroic deeds of those who had lived on earth before them.

So pleasant was the life that no one spared a thought for the men and women who still dwelt on earth, struggling to eke out a living in the cold and the rain and the gales, and so contented were the birds with their lot that they sang only of their happiness in the Land of Youth, all except one small bird – the redstart.

Now the redstart was – as indeed it still is – a shy bird, with a soft, rather sad song which revealed, even in those far-off days,

47

that it remembered all was not well with the men and women on earth and was concerned for them.

At last, unable to enjoy the peace of Tir-nan-Og because of the thought of the suffering of mankind, she flew to the god of the Land of Youth.

"In the rain-swept islands of the Hebrides, the people huddle together in little huts, with only poor garments woven from the wool of sheep or made from the skins of animals to keep them warm, and they eat raw shellfish and grain because they have no means of cooking their food. Let me take fire to them, O Great One."

The god considered the request.

"Fire is the most precious gift you could ask of me, little redstart," he said at length. "I shall give it to you, however, because I know how you care for others, but before you in turn can give it to those who dwell on the earth you must first find one person who is like yourself – kind and good and unselfish."

"I am sure that will not be difficult," the redstart answered happily and watched as the god placed on her tail a spark of perpetual fire.

Away she flew from the warmth and sunshine of Tir-nan-Og, over the storm-tossed waves and through the mists and spray, until at last she landed on the shore of a rocky island where men were hunting in the pools for shellfish and seaweed and such small fish and crabs as had been left behind by the tide.

"I have flown all the way from Tir-nan-Og with the gift of fire so that you can keep yourself and your family warm and cook that fish you have just caught," the redstart said, coming to rest on a boulder beside one of the fishermen, but he did not know what fire was and was too stupid to listen to what the bird was telling him.

"What a miserable little bird you are! Once I've plucked off your feathers you will be even smaller, but even so you should make one mouthful of tender eating," he grunted, and picking up a stone he threw it at the redstart and would have killed her had she not flown off in fright.

Again and again the bird approached different men, offering them the gift of fire, but so selfish were they and so concerned with their own affairs that no one would listen to her, and each man in his greed and hunger tried to kill her.

At last, filled with despair, she flew to an abandoned croft to seek help from the owl who lived there and whom she knew to be the wisest of all the birds.

"The god of Tir-nan-Og has given me a spark of perpetual fire for the people of this earth on condition that I can find someone who is kind and good and unselfish. How can I find such a person when everyone I approach tries to kill me?"

After due consideration, the owl summoned to the croft all the birds of the Hebrides and the stormy seas which surrounded them – the gulls and kittiwakes and terns, the guillemots, fulmars and storm petrels, the wild ducks, geese and swans, the cormorants and gannets and the plovers and sweet-singing larks.

"I want you to fly all over the earth," the owl said to the assembled birds, "and let every man know that the redstart has flown from Tir-nan-Og with the precious gift of fire, to be given to whoever amongst them is kind and good and unselfish."

Away the birds flew, and presently men began to hurry to the abandoned croft where the redstart waited with the owl. Each man claimed that the gift was for him alone, as only he was kind and good and unselfish. Angrier and angrier grew the men and louder and louder grew the clamour, until before long they were fighting amongst themselves and the air was filled with the ugly sounds of battle and the groans of injured men.

"This is no place for you or for me," the owl said. "I suggest you return at once to Tir-nan-Og as there is no one worthy of the gift you have to offer." And away he flew to the safety of the nearest wood.

Weary from the distance she had already flown and saddened by her treatment at the hands of men, the redstart set off, battling against the wind and drenched by the rain, until at last, utterly exhausted, she collapsed on the sandy shore of Islay. In vain she tried to make for shelter amongst the nearby bog-myrtle and heather; she was too weak and hungry to fly any further, and closing her eyes, she lay there, terrified and trembling.

Presently a little boy came running across the sand and stopped suddenly.

"Poor wee thing," he said, picking up the redstart and stroking her gently with his forefinger. "The sea birds are big and strong and can battle against the storms, but you are so small and have no strength left in you at all." And he carried the bird back to the heather-thatched hut where his brothers and sisters were playing and his mother was singing softly to the baby in her arms.

"Poor wee thing," the mother said. "Keep her warm in your hands for a little while, then give her water to drink and curds to eat."

When the redstart was warm once more and had sipped the water and been fed the curds, she told the mother of her long journey from Tir-nan-Og with her gift of fire.

"Are you good and kind and unselfish?" she asked hopefully.

The mother looked up from the baby she was nursing and shook her head.

"Why do you ask me, little bird? I have so much to do while my husband is away hunting or fishing.

"I nurse the baby and care for the children and feed them and have something ready for my husband when he comes home at night. I spin and weave and make clothes for us all. I dig the ground to grow food and search the moors for berries and the woods for nuts. No, little bird, I have no time to be good or kind or unselfish."

When the mother had finished speaking, the redstart was filled with great happiness, for she knew that at last she had found someone worthy of her precious gift.

"Can you find me a large flat stone and place it on the floor in the middle of the hut?" she asked the boy.

"Of course I can," the boy answered, and off he went with his brothers and sisters to the seashore, to return in no time at all with exactly the right size of flat stone, which they placed on the floor in the middle of the hut.

"Can you build me a nest of pine twigs on that stone?" the redstart asked next.

"Of course I can," the boy answered, and off he ran with his brothers and sisters to gather fallen twigs from the forest nearby.

Carefully the boy built a nest of pine twigs on the flat stone and the redstart fluttered gently down on to it.

As soon as the spark of fire had set alight to the resin in the twigs, the redstart, now strong and happy, flew away through the open door and over the grey stormy seas, back to the blue skies and green fields of Tir-nan-Og, the Land of Youth.

As for the fire that was kindled in the nest of pine twigs in the hut, it was never allowed to go out, and because the mother was good and kind and unselfish without ever realizing it, she let it be known that anyone who cared could bring a pine branch and carry fire back to his own home.

And that – so the mothers of Islay used to say – is how mankind first received fire and how the redstart even to this day carries on her tail a red streak like a spark of perpetual fire.

Whuppity Stoorie

There once lived a goodman, his wife and bairn in the hamlet of Kittlerumpit in the Debatable Lands, which lay in the Border Country between England and Scotland.

Now early one morning the goodman set off for the local fair with produce from his croft, and as always he bade his wife have nothing to do with Wise Women, Little People or hobgoblins, because it was well-known that such creatures were bad-tempered and spiteful and nothing delighted them more than to cause misery and unhappiness.

When night fell and the goodman had not returned, his wife, deciding he must have lingered to drink and talk with his friends, shut up the hens, the sow and the goats, fed the bairn and went to sleep.

At the first light of morning there was a loud knocking at the front door, and looking out of the bedroom window, she saw the miller's son standing there, a sack of flour in his arms.

"My father sent me to tell ye that the press-gang were at the fair yestre'en and they took your man for a sailor," he said. And he put the sack of flour on the step and ran back to the mill as fast as his legs would carry him.

"Oh, dear! Oh, dear! Oh, dear!" the goodwife cried. "The press-gang have taken my man for a sailor and I may never see him again. Whatever is to become of me and my bairn? Shall I weep now or later?"

Just then the bairn in the cradle began to cry because it was hungry, the hens and goats demanded to be let out and the sow in the sty grunted loudly for food, and so the goodwife dressed herself quickly, and by the time she had cared for bairn, hens,

53

goats and sow, cleaned her cottage and baked some bannocks, there was no time left for weeping.

Although her neighbours were poor and all had their share of misfortunes, they were sorry for the goodwife and took it in turn to spare her something for the pot, to cut wood for the fire and to dig the croft so that she could grow corn and oats and cabbages and beans.

One evening, when she was gathering fallen branches for firewood in the forest nearby, the bairn snug in a shawl on her back, she came across a hare caught in a trap by its hind leg.

"Exactly what I want for my stock pot," she cried, and was just going to wring the creature's neck when she saw the sad look in its eyes as it stared past her to the bairn on her back.

"And who will look after my bairns now that the hunter has shot their father and you are about to wring my neck?" the hare asked.

The goodwife hesitated.

And sighed.

"Go back to your bairns," she said at length, and she released the trap. But the hare's leg was broken and it could not run away. "I have done all I can," the goodwife declared and would have hurried away had not the bairn on her back begun to whimper.

"There is little that I can do," she said to the hare, "but that little I will do." She looked along the verge of the forest until she found some comfrey, and then, pulling up the plant, she set to work with a sharp stone to shred the juicy root on to the corner of her kerchief: this she bound on to the hare's leg, knowing that the comfrey would set like a plaster and the broken limb would heal perfectly.

Without a word of thanks the hare limped out of sight, and with only a momentary pang of regret for the stew she might have had, the goodwife began to gather nettle-tops, bracken, sorrel and Jock-by-the-hedge, deciding that if she added some of her stock of dried peas and bacon rind, she would have a meal fit for a queen.

Time passed, and just when it seemed as though she could manage on her own and when she dared to hope that sooner or later her goodman would return to her somehow, the sow, which was due to farrow any day, fell sick and nothing that the goodwife could do was of any avail.

She spoke to it soothingly and tempted it with a mash of beech nuts and acorns, but the sow lay on its back and closed its eyes and struggled with every breath it drew.

"Oh dear! Oh, dear! Oh, dear!" the goodwife cried, sitting down on the knocking stone. "The sow is dying and all her litter of fine piglets will die with her too. Shall I weep now or later?"

Just then the bairn in the shawl on her back began to chuckle and gurgle, and turning round, the goodwife saw a strange old lady walking up the brae towards her: she was dressed in green and wore a white apron and a high-crowned hat, and she carried a walking stick as tall as she was herself.

Curtseying to the old lady in green, the goodwife would have poured out all her troubles, had not the stranger held up her hand for silence.

"I know about your sow," she said in a shrill voice. "Why do ye think I am here if not to help ye? Tell me – what will ye give me if I cure it?"

"Give ye, fine lady? Why, I will give ye anything ye like," the goodwife answered, never stopping to think what it was she was saying, so upset and flustered was she.

With a smile of satisfaction the old lady in green entered the sty and from the pocket in her white apron she drew a little bottle; sprinkling the contents on the sow's ears, snout and the tip of its tail, she muttered something beneath her breath, something which sounded like:

> Pitter, patter
> Holy watter.
> Get up, sow,
> Ye're weel now.

Immediately the sow got to its feet, grunted and walked across to enjoy the mash it had refused only a short time before.

"However can I thank ye?" the goodwife cried, her eyes sparkling with joy.

"Easily enough. Ye promised me anything I wanted. All I want is your bairn."

"My bairn, fine lady?" Reaching for the child on her back, the goodwife clutched it to her in distress. Only now did she realize it was no ordinary human being she was talking to: too late she remembered how her husband had warned her to have nothing to do with Wise Women, Little People or hobgoblins, because nothing delighted them more than to cause misery and unhappiness. "Not my bairn, sweet lady. Anything else, but not my bairn."

The old lady scowled and brandished her staff.

"By my magic I healed your sow when it would have died and now ye must bide by your word. Give me the bonny bairn."

Hastily the goodwife recalled what she knew of fairy lore.

"I gave my word and it is true that I must bide by it, fine lady, but ye must give me three days and if I can find out your name in that time, then ye lose all claim to my bairn."

Now the old lady in green was so angry that she would have struck the goodwife with her staff had not a black crow flown out of the wood and frightened her by its squawking.

"Three days," the old lady agreed sullenly, "but if it were three years ye would never find out my name," and turning, she hurried down the brae and out of sight.

"Oh, dear! Oh, dear! Oh, dear!" the goodwife cried as she hurried back into her cottage. "Whatever is to become of me and my bonny bairn? Shall I weep now or later?"

Just then the bairn in her arms began to kick and struggle and the goodwife had to soothe and tend to it, and by the time she had shut up the hens and goat, spoken reassuringly to the sow and eaten her supper, she was so tired that she went straight to bed and fell fast asleep.

When she awoke the next morning, she knew what she had to do. With bread and cheese in her pocket and the bairn on her back, she called at all the cottages of Kittlerumpit and at the nearby farms as well as the mill by the stream, but no one there had ever heard of the old lady in green or knew her name.

The second day she walked to homesteads farther afield, but the farmers, their wives and their hired help all shook their heads and said they too had never heard of the old lady in green or knew her name.

Tired, footsore and weary, the goodwife returned to her cottage at nightfall and was walking through her herb garden,

where she grew clary and follow-me-lad, sage and rosemary, thyme and tansy and many other plants which she used to flavour her simple meals, when suddenly a hare jumped out in front of her.

"Do you remember me?" it asked.

Looking at the healing comfrey plaster, still bound with the corner of her kerchief, the goodwife nodded her head.

"One good turn deserves another. Tonight, when the moon shows over the pine forest, go softly to the spring at the bottom of the old quarry and ye shall hear what will gladden your heart." And the hare disappeared amongst the plants of the herb garden before the goodwife could stammer her thanks.

Patiently she waited until the moon showed over the pine forest and then she set off, soft-footed, through the lonely countryside. When at last she reached the edge of the quarry, she fell to her knees and peered over the edge and to her amazement she saw the old lady in green sitting by the spring, spinning busily, and as the wheel whirred round and round she sang triumphantly:

> Little kens our good dame at hame
> That Whuppity Stoorie is my name.

Scarcely able to contain her delight, the goodwife crept home as quietly as she had come, and slept soundly and at peace until first light.

When she got up she found that the sow now had a litter of twelve healthy piglets and was lying on its side, grunting with pride and satisfaction. Relieved and thankful, the goodwife tended her stock, cleaned her cottage, and then, wrapping her bairn warmly in three shawls, carried it out and hid it near the knocking stone. Sitting down on the stone, she spread out her skirts, smoothed her apron, and waited.

It was almost midday when the old lady in green came walking up the brae towards her, the high-crowned hat on her head, the walking stick as tall as herself in one hand.

"I cured your sow and now I've come for your bairn," she said sharply.

"No one could be so unfeeling and cruel as to take another woman's bairn, fine lady," the goodwife said. "Will ye not be content with the sow and all her fine piglets instead?"

"It was the bairn ye promised, not the sow and its piglets," the old lady in green replied angrily.

"Think again," the goodwife begged. "Will ye not take me instead?"

"And what good would the likes of ye be to me?" the lady in green demanded, fire flashing from her eyes. "Give me the bairn that ye have hidden behind the knocking stone or it will be the worse for ye."

Slowly the goodwife rose from the stone where she sat and curtseyed to the irate fairy.

"I should have known better than to accept a kindness from a fine lady of the name of Whuppity Stoorie," she said.

With a scream of baffled rage the fairy leaped three times her height into the air and then fled down the brae and was never seen again.

As for the goodwife, she loved her bairn and tended her croft and in good time her husband secured his release from the Navy and came back to her with many an exciting tale to tell of his adventures at sea, but none was as exciting as the tale she had to tell him of the fine lady called Whuppity Stoorie, who tried so hard to steal away their own dear bairn.

Callaly Castle

The hounds entered first, panting and mud bespattered. With noisy gulps they drank the water from the trough at the door and then, bounding over the rush-strewn floor, they collapsed with a thud under the table. Sighing softly, the lady of Callaly Castle watched the smoke from the fire in the centre of the great hall spread all over the room, instead of rising straight up to the hole in the roof which served as a chimney.

The retainers came in next – those who had taken a toss as liberally smeared with Northumbrian mud as the hounds and all of them smelling of honest sweat. Again the smoke swirled and eddied and sank.

The lord of Callaly came last, his arm thrown carelessly round the shoulders of his youngest son, while the two older ones followed behind. One quick glance through the smoke-filled hall told the lady all she needed to know. The sport had gone well that day. There would be fresh meat in the pantry for several weeks to come, and from the quick smiles her sons gave her, she knew they had all seized their chance to talk to their father.

Lifting her hand, she signalled to the servants to bring in the wooden tub and fill it with water, and while her lord bathed in front of the fire she listened, with every appearance of interest, as he described in detail just how successful the day's hunting had been.

It was only when the grooms came in after seeing to the horses, and the draught from the open door blew smoke out all over the lord so that he coughed and choked and swore, that he remembered the wonderful idea which had occurred to him when he was chasing the deer on the wooded slopes of the Cheviot Hills.

"Put the shutters up at the windows," he shouted. "A man deserves some comfort in his own castle after a hard day in the saddle."

"The shutters are all broken and twisted after the gales of February fill-dyke, my lord," his steward reminded him.

"What a way to live!" the lord exclaimed, as his page rubbed him dry and held out clean hose and linen and his favourite padded tunic, edged with fur. "Windows which are nothing but holes in the walls through which the winds blow and the rain and snow drive, and a fire which smokes every time the door is opened and quite often when it is closed.

"This castle may have been good enough for my father and my grandfather and all my ancestors," he continued, looking at his wife, "but for some time I have been thinking that we could afford something a little more – er – how exactly can I put it?"

"Something which is rather more suitable for a man of your rank, wealth and outstanding personality," his wife suggested.

"Exactly. Just because we live in Northumberland, that does not mean that we have not heard of new ideas. Where was that place someone was telling me about where the fire is at the end of the hall, with a big hood over it, and the smoke goes up a wide chimney instead of blowing all over the place? And are not the windows filled with fine horn which lets in the light and keeps out the wind and rain?"

"That was Alnwick Castle," his wife answered. "Of course the Percys there are much wealthier than you and can afford all manner of improvements. I have heard, however, that the Ridleys are rebuilding and are thinking of having glass in their windows, as they do in our churches, but that I think would cost a great deal of money indeed."

"Rebuilding, are they?" the lord said thoughtfully. "Glass in the windows? Ridiculous! But if they can afford it, then I certainly can. Yes. I have made up my mind. I shall build a new castle. Tomorrow I shall send for my masons and craftsmen, my joiners and carpenters and discuss every new idea with them."

"Well done, my brave sons," the lady of the castle murmured as the lord, tired out by his day's exercise, withdrew to the curtained off corner of the hall which contained their bed.

The boys smiled back, each pleased at the way he had managed, quite casually, to interest his father in the idea of building a new and comfortable home for his mother who suffered, without ever complaining, from the damp and icy draughts of the old castle.

Day after day, the lord talked with his masons and plasterers, his joiners and carpenters, his blacksmiths and foresters, discussing where the stone for the new castle was to be quarried, what seasoned wood there was in store and which trees should be felled in addition. Each evening he would inform his wife what had been decided and each morning he would arise with new and better ideas which had occurred to him from some hint dropped by one of his family – ideas which included carved furniture, panelling on the walls, plasterwork on the ceiling and feather beds instead of straw to sleep on.

All was going splendidly and the lady of Callaly Castle was just congratulating herself that at last she would have a home which was exactly what she had always wanted, when her husband strode in, his cheeks red from the blustering wind.

"That is settled," he cried, standing in front of the fire and swaying gently back and forward. "At last I've decided on the site for our new castle. It was not easy, as there were many things to be taken into consideration. You do not know how fortunate you are to sit at home, weaving by the fire, untroubled by all the work involved in building a new castle."

"Of course I know how fortunate I am to have such a clever and thoughtful husband," the lady answered, looking admiringly at the lord. "You have no idea how wonderful it will be for me to live in a castle protected from the north-east gales by the hills, and to have the howl of the wind muted by the trees. And at last I shall be able to have a herb garden and to grow fruit as well."

"Herb garden? Fruit? On the top of that hill?" With a laugh the lord pointed to the steep wooded hill which they could see through the window.

"On the top of the hill?" his wife repeated in dismay. "But I thought you had decided there was only one possible place for your new castle, and that was on the level ground of Shepherd's Shaw." And she pointed down to the pleasant valley below.

"No, it was you who decided that," the lord answered brusquely, and not all his wife's hints or the suggestions of his sons could make him alter his mind.

On the top of the hill the foundations were dug and the walls began to rise, and every time the lady looked out of the window she heaved a deep sigh.

If only something would happen to make him change his mind, she thought one evening, when the lord had gone to see a neighbour about some boundary dispute and her sons were gathered round her, talking idly.

"Did you hear the groom talking last night about some castle where he had worked?" the eldest son asked. "He said that a monk had been slain there many years ago and that ever since the grounds have been haunted by a ghost which walks around all night, groaning most fearfully, so that no one will venture out after nightfall."

"But the scullion's tale was even better," the second son said. "He comes from a place where there is a terrible creature called a barguest, who pounces on lonely travellers, and so terrible is his appearance that he frightens them to death. He swears that he personally knew of a man who saw this barguest and died within the hour."

"The steward says there are far worse creatures than barguests in the Cheviot Hills here," the youngest son said. "I heard him telling the others that fearful demons with skins covered with fur, and with long tails and claws dripping with blood, roam the hills looking for solitary wayfarers whom they tear to pieces and devour."

"I hope you do not believe such nonsense," the lady said with a little smile.

"Of course not," they all answered together.

"What a pity no dreadful creature haunts the hill where our new castle is being built," the eldest boy said lightly. "If it did you would never get any of our men to work there."

There was a long silence.

"If such a creature did exist," the lady said idly, "I wonder if it would look anything like that great bear my cousin's husband killed last year? She meant to use the skin on their bed, but it was not properly cured and had such an offensive smell that she gave it to their chief huntsman instead. It is quite possible that he would be willing to part with it for a consideration."

Opening the purse which hung at her girdle, she took out some coins and gave them to her eldest son.

"It should not take you long to ride to Cartington Castle," she said. "Have a word privately with the huntsman, and if he is willing to sell the skin, tell him to say nothing to anyone else about the matter."

"One bearskin?" the youngest son asked. "Three would be better."

"One is enough," his mother answered. "There will be plenty of hard work for the three of you to plant the seeds of fear, but when the time comes, only one will be needed – he who is tallest and strongest and has the deepest voice."

"And that is me," the eldest son said, and off he rode to Cartington and was back before nightfall with the ill-smelling bearskin over his saddle.

The next morning when the workmen reached the top of the hill they halted, aghast. Large portions of the walls which they had been building so carefully for weeks had been pulled down, and the stones lay scattered among the nettles and briars.

"I always said it was too windy to build up here," one of the men muttered. "My ague has been twice as bad since I started working on the top of this hill."

"There was no wind last night," his fellow objected. "It dropped at sunset, just as we stopped work."

"If you ask me," a third man said, looking around fearfully, "this place is haunted. My wife's mother says this is the home of some evil spirit. She said we would have trouble if we tried to build here. And we have. Who was it that struck the carpenter with palsy yesterday so that he could not hold his tools? And what caused the mason's apprentice to drop that stone and crush his foot so that he is unable to walk? I tell you, if we go on working here, we shall pay for it with our lives."

"And who will tell our lord that we are too frightened to go on working at his new castle?" the master mason demanded.

"At all events, he ought to come and see for himself what has happened," the first man insisted.

So the master mason went for the lord, and when he climbed up and saw the fallen walls he was very angry.

"They were not built properly," he stormed. "Men do not know how to do an honest day's work these days. Get on with your work at once. Today I shall stay here and make sure everything is done properly."

That day the men worked harder than ever, repairing the damage and they returned to their homes tired and weary that night. And it was just as well that the lord had been out from sunrise to sunset and did not know that his three sons had slept most of the day in front of the fire in the great hall.

The following morning, when the workmen reached the top of the hill, they could not believe their eyes. All the previous day's work was undone and this time the stones were scattered and hurled far down the hillside.

Again the lord was sent for, but this time he could not blame his men as he himself had supervised them all day.

Can I have an enemy who is doing this to me, he wondered. But he had no quarrel with his neighbours, and if he had, they would have settled the matter by fighting and certainly would not steal out at night and knock down his castle walls.

Mystified and worried, he ordered his men to start work again, but scarcely had they begun than the sky darkened, thunder rolled and lightning flashed over the Cheviots and he was very conscious of the frightened looks his workmen cast over their shoulders. His uneasiness increased when he overheard one man whisper to another that it was his opinion that they had disturbed the old gods who had lived in the hill ever since the days of their forefathers, and they would have their revenge on every one of them.

Down poured the rain so incessantly that at last the lord told his men to abandon the work before half the walls were rebuilt, and great was his annoyance when, soaked to the skin, he strode into the great hall to find his sons asleep by the fire.

He was just going to stir them, none too gently, with the toe of his boot, when his wife intervened.

"Let them rest," she begged. "I am worried about them and have given them a soothing draught. Ever since the first day when they went up with you to see the men start building our new castle, they have been tired and listless. Sometimes I wonder if they have been bewitched, and at others I feel it is all some kind of dreadful warning. Now with this business of the walls being pulled down at night, I fear for them, and even more for you, my lord. It seems to me that you are not looking quite as well as you usually do."

The lord frowned.

"I must confess I do not feel in such good health as usual," he admitted.

"Some mulled ale, well-spiced, would be of great help, especially if any witchcraft is involved," the lady said, signing to one of her maids to prepare the drink.

"Old gods disturbed, witchcraft, dreadful warnings!" the lord cried. "I am going to get to the bottom of this. Tonight I shall keep watch on the hill." And he sneezed violently.

"Oh, no," the lady cried in alarm. "Whatever the creature is that has been disturbed, the sight of you would surely provoke it to attack you. Send a couple of your men and bid them hide behind the great elm tree: there they can see everything without being seen themselves. In the morning they can report to you and then you can decide what action to take."

"Perhaps you are right," the lord agreed, sneezing again. "Whom do you suggest I should send?"

"The steward, perhaps? And one of your bravest men-at-arms?"

"I shall tell them immediately," the lord said.

Towards evening the thunder died away and the lightning ceased but the rain continued to pour down steadily. None too happily the steward and one of the men-at-arms left the castle just before midnight and groped and stumbled up to the old elm tree.

"Now what are we supposed to do?" the man-at-arms grumbled. "It is much too dark to see anything."

"Perhaps that is just as well," the steward muttered, remembering the fearful demons with skins covered with fur, and with long tails and claws dripping with blood.

Suddenly they heard a shriek so terrible that their blood ran cold.

And then they saw it.

It was a sight which neither of them was ever to forget: one

which they were to tell over and over again to their children and grandchildren and great-grandchildren.

On the top of the wall which had been rebuilt only that morning, a great shaggy creature appeared, the flaming torch in its hand lighting up its glittering eyes, its cruel teeth and long, curved claws. With a hoarse laugh it knelt, seized on of the stones and hurled it down the hillside and then shrieked again.

Although the men were hidden by the tree, the creature seemed to sense where they were, for turning, it pointed in their direction and shouted hoarsely:

> Callaly Castle built on the height,
> Up in the day and down in the night.
> Builded down in the Shepherd's Shaw
> It shall stand for aye and never fa'.

It was enough for the two watchers, and more than enough. With wild cries of terror they turned and blundered downhill, bursting into the great hall with such moans and cries that everyone, including the lord and lady, woke up and demanded to know what was the matter.

So great was the commotion and scurrying around and preparing of hot ale for the steward and the man-at-arms and everyone else, that no one noticed the eldest son slip in and take his place by his brothers.

"Horrible, horrible," the steward moaned. "A great shaggy creature like a bear, only twice as big."

"Three times," the man-at-arms interrupted.

"Three times as big," the steward agreed. "With eyes like glowing fires –"

"– and seven rows of teeth and a long forked tail," the man-at-arms added. He had always had a good imagination.

"And what was it you said the creature shouted at you?" the lady asked.

Both men drew deep breaths and recited together:

> Callaly Castle built on the height,
> Up in the day and down in the night.
> Builded down in the Shepherd's Shaw
> It shall stand for aye and never fa'.

68

"We have disturbed some creature from the underworld and we shall never succeed in building the castle on the hill," someone said.

"It may well be that this is a sign from heaven to guide you to the right place," the lady said softly.

A sign from heaven sounded much better than being chased away by some creature from the underworld, the lord thought, and there and then he announced that he had always wondered if the hill was the best place for his new castle. Personally he had favoured the Shepherd's Shaw, but others had persuaded him against it. Now he was going to have his own way for once and tomorrow they would start building down in the valley.

And that is exactly what they did.

And if you go to Callaly in Northumberland, there on the top of the hill you will see the remains of the castle the lord started to build before his wife and sons played their trick on him, and down on the Shepherd's Shaw you will see what is left of the new castle which the lord built and in which he and his wife and family lived for many a long year.

Columba and the Water-horse

Long, long ago, before Columba had built his monastery on the island of Iona or had sent his Men of God to the Western Highlands of Scotland to tell the people about the Christ Child, there dwelt in that land of high mountains, deep lochs and lonely glens all manner of creatures – witches and wizards, Little People and giants, mermaids and seal folk . . . and water-horses.

Now a water-horse, to all appearances, looked just like any ordinary horse as he cropped the green grass beside the reed-fringed loch where he lived, but as everyone in those days knew, he differed from an ordinary horse in two important ways: his home was underneath the chill waters on the very bed of the loch, and he had the gift of changing himself, whenever he pleased, into a handsome young man.

Some water-horses feared and disliked human beings and did all they could to harm them; some were content to live their own lives as long as men and women kept out of their way, while a few loved the ordinary people and were loved by them in return.

Among those who delighted in the company of human beings was a water-horse called Garth. He was a splendid creature, as white as the spray the west wind whipped on the surface of the Loch of the Seven Birch Trees, where he lived; his coat was as smooth to the touch as the finest silk, his mane as glossy as a maiden's hair, while his bridle was fashioned from the rarest red-gold and set with amethysts, jet and fresh-water pearls.

At such times as he took on human form, Garth was tall and broad in the shoulder; his skin was as white as the big-cotton, his cheeks as red as the rowan berry and his hair as yellow as the ripening corn.

When he first came to live in the Loch of the Seven Birch Trees the fishermen, farmers and hunters who lived nearby were ill-pleased, because they knew that many water-horses hated men and women and delighted in carrying them off and drowning them in the deep loch waters. But it was not long before they realized that Garth loved all creatures, human and fairy, and that most of all he loved children.

Nothing gave him greater pleasure than to hear the boys and girls running from their homes through the marshes scented with myrtle and woodruff and thyme, and racing to the edge of the loch where they would stand and call,

"Garth! Garth! Please come and play with us."

At the sound of their voices he would rise from his home at the bottom of the loch and gallop through the sedges and tall reeds to the waiting children. Laughing and excited, they would climb on to his back – and it did not matter how many children awaited him, there was always room for every one of them – and then he would be off.

Through the quaking bogs and peat hags he would gallop, into the pine forests which clothed the lower slopes of the mountains, and out and on to the bare red-brown rocks, and up and up until he reached the snow-covered peak, where the crisp air would ring with the children's joyful laughter as they looked down at the world of forest and lakes and desolate moors spread out around them. When at last they had had their fill of looking, Garth would take them back, safe and happy, to the shores of the loch where first they had called to him.

Another time, when perhaps he was basking in the thin autumn sunshine, he might see a poor woman bent under the weight of the load of peat she was carrying back to her cottage; then he would gallop up to her, and when she had mounted him he would amble gently along with his burden, neighing happily when she tried to thank him.

More than one fisherman owed his life to Garth, for in a matter of moments tremendous winds could arise, striking the loch in violent squalls which whipped the waters into dangerous whirlpools. At such times Garth would come to the surface and, assuming human form, would climb into the frail tossing fishing-

boat and, straining at the oars, would help the fishermen to the safety of the shore.

With the passing of the years the children who had ridden Garth grew up, married and had children of their own, and they in turn had children, and grandchildren, and great-grandchildren, and always the little ones loved Garth, and raced through the marshes to the shore of the loch, calling to him to come and play with them, and always he answered their call.

So he lived in peace and great contentment until one day the youngest son of Iain the Hunter flung his arms round Garth's neck, crying,

"How good you are to us, Garth, and how lucky we are that the only water-horse in the land should live near us in the Loch of the Seven Birch Trees."

"But every loch in the land has its water-horse," Garth said.

"Not now," the little boy answered.

"Not now," the children who were with him agreed.

"Then what has happened to them?" Garth asked.

72

"The Men of God say there is no place for water-horses or witches, for fairies or giants, and they have all gone back to Tir-nan-Og, the Land of Youth."

"Who are these Men of God that they should say such things?" Garth demanded angrily.

. "They are very good men who even now are building their House of Stone on the top of the Hill of the Tumbled Rocks."

"But the Hill of the Tumbled Rocks belongs to the Little People," Garth said. "They will punish anyone who tries to build there or disturb them in any way."

"Not any longer," the son of Iain the Hunter replied. "The Men of God have banished the Little People from this land too. Those who are brave enough to stay here must dwell underground and appear only at night, when we are all asleep."

Throughout the whole of the night Garth thought about what the children had told him, and the next day he waited for them to come down to the shores of the loch so that he could ask more about these Men of God who were so powerful that they could banish from their homes creatures who had lived there time out of mind.

But no children came to the loch that day, and the only sound was the lapping of the grey water among the dead reeds.

And no children came the day after, and the only sounds were the lapping of the grey water and the lament of the curlew overhead.

On the third day, however, just as dawn was breaking, the youngest son of Iain the Hunter appeared beside the frozen reeds and called softly,

"Garth! Garth!"

When the water-horse stood beside him, the little boy gazed at him sadly.

"My father and my mother think that I am still asleep," he whispered, "but I had to come to say good-bye to you, dear Garth."

"Good-bye?" Garth said in a puzzled voice. "Are you going away then?"

The little boy shook his head and his eyes filled with tears.

"Oh, no. But the Men of God have finished building their house on the Hill of the Tumbled Rocks, though they call it a church and not a house. Tomorrow Columba – who is the greatest and wisest of them all – is coming here from the island of Iona to welcome us to this church and to talk to us. You see, tomorrow is a very special day for the Men of God, because it is the anniversary of the day when the Christ Child was born, the Child who taught people to love one another.

"And the Men of God have told our parents that after tomorrow none of us must play with you or ride on your back, and because our parents must now obey the Men of God and we must obey our parents, that is why I have come to say good-bye to you."

The little boy hugged Garth, stroked the red-gold bridle set with amethysts, jet and fresh-water pearls and, turning away with a sob, ran back across the marsh to his home.

Who are these Men of God, and why should they take the children from me, Garth thought sadly. All day he went over what the little boy had said and by nightfall he had made up his mind what he must do.

The next morning he swam to the surface of the loch and as soon as he had gained the bank he changed himself into a young man, his skin as white as the bog cotton, his cheeks as red as the rowan berry and his hair as yellow as the ripening corn, and he set off for the Hill of the Tumbled Rocks.

It was a long time since he had been that way, and in spite of what the youngest son of Iain the Hunter had told him, he was amazed to find that where once the Little People had danced there was now a strange building, not made of clay and straw and roofed with branches of trees and heather like the homes of the fishermen, farmers and hunters – no! This building was made of stone and it had two narrow windows, and one wall was raised above the rest and in it hung a bell which rang out in the frosty air, summoning the people from all around.

Hiding behind a whin bush, Garth watched the people he knew so well – men, women and children – enter the stone building. Presently he heard the sound of mouth music and then a voice he had never heard before began to speak, telling the people about the Christ Child who had been born long ago in a place called Bethlehem and how, when this Child grew up, he taught all people to love one another and worship the one true God.

When at last the voice stopped, the door was opened and out came two men who were strangers to Garth. Although one was much older than the other, both were dressed alike in long robes of coarsely woven cloth tied at the waist with knotted rope: despite the cold weather both wore open sandals on their bare feet, while in their left hands each carried a staff fashioned from the wood of the wild cherry.

So those are the Men of God, Garth thought, watching as they made a strange sign over each person who had been in the stone building: they seem to me to be just like other men, and as I have done them no harm, then surely they can wish me no ill.

Rising from his hiding place, he walked across to the strangers, and the people parted and made way for him, and although they all knew who he was, not one of them spoke to him.

"I have lived long in this country of mountains and lochs and mists and rain and the glory of the setting sun," he said, addressing the younger of the two Men of God, "and I have

75

known many gods but have wanted to worship none until I heard you speak this morning of the Christ Child who taught that all people and all creatures should love one another. Will you allow me to join these people whom I know and worship your one true God?"

Long and hard the younger Man of God stared at Garth until, recognizing him for what he was, anger clouded his face.

"A water-horse!" he cried. "There is no more hope of a water-horse joining these people and worshipping the one true God than there is of this old staff bearing new blossom!" In great wrath he brought down his staff so violently that it sank into the ground in front of him. "Begone!" he cried. "There is no place for you and the likes of you now in this land."

"But what wrong have I done?" Garth pleaded. "I have always loved all men and all creatures."

"Begone!" the Man of God repeated, and so terrible was his anger that Garth felt all his old magic drain from him so that he changed back into a water-horse, wearing his red-gold bridle set with amethysts, jet and fresh-water pearls, and the gift of speech left him so that he could only look with sad, grey eyes at the Man of God and then turn away, not knowing where to go or what to do.

"Wait!" a voice commanded, and the older of the two men stepped forward, and Garth, turning, knew that he was face to face with Columba of Iona, the greatest and wisest of all the Men of God.

Looking into the eyes of the water-horse, Columba saw only kindness and humility, and he felt a great pity for Garth, knowing that he was left over from a world older than his. Sensing this pity, the people pressed close, eager to tell Columba how good Garth had been to them and their parents and grandparents and great-grandparents, and the air was filled with passionate pleas that the Men of God should not send Garth from them, until suddenly the childish voice of the youngest son of Iain the Hunter rang out.

"Look!" he cried. "Oh, look!"

Turning, everyone fell silent, staring in wonder and amazement. The staff, which the younger Man of God had thrust so angrily into the ground on that chill December day, had taken root and put out branches, and the branches were covered with the delicate white flowers which the wild cherry bears in the springtime.

"There is no need for any of you to tell me more about Garth," Columba declared. "The Christ Child has accepted him in His own way."

As Columba spoke, Garth resumed his human form – which he was to keep to the end of his days – and in his hand he carried the bridle which was fashioned from the finest red-gold and set with amethysts, jet and fresh-water pearls.

"When I lived in the Old World," he said, "this was my most precious possession: now that you have accepted me into your world, I want you to have it to do with as you will."

Columba smiled as he accepted the beautiful bridle, while the younger Man of God, who in his youthful pride and ignorance would have turned Garth away, was humbled and ashamed even though Garth forgave him freely.

Later, when Columba returned to his monastery on the island of Iona, he took Garth with him and taught him all about the Christ Child and the one true God. After that Garth accompanied him on his journeys all over the mainland, and wherever they went children flocked to listen to Garth as he told them of the Child who was born in Bethlehem and whose name is Love.

And as long as Garth lived, no matter how wild the storm, how chill the wind, how deep the snow, every Christmas morning the wild cherry blossomed in front of the church on the Hill of the Tumbled Rocks, to remind all those who journeyed thither over the high mountains and through the passes and over the moors, how great is the power of Love.

The Three Golden Heads

In olden times before King Arthur ruled the land, there lived a King of Colchester who had everything a man could desire – land and riches, a good wife whom everyone loved and a kind and beautiful daughter.

When his daughter was about fifteen, the queen died, and the king, not content with all the wealth that was already his, married again, choosing a woman who, though rich, was ugly and spiteful and who possessed an ugly and spiteful daughter.

The second wife, wanting her own ugly daughter to be the most important princess in the land, did everything in her power to make her step-daughter unhappy and to turn her father against her.

Constantly she praised her own daughter and told such lies about her step-daughter that at last the king declared he would have nothing more to do with his own child, and refused to let her eat with him in the hall or walk with him in the palace gardens.

Not content with the harm she had already done, the step-mother set the girl menial tasks to do and bade her eat with the servants and sleep in an attic where the wind blew through the crevices and the rain dripped through the roof.

So unhappy was the princess that one day, seeing her father walking in the garden, she hurried forward and knelt in front of him.

"There is no place for me here in Colchester," she said sadly. "Grant me permission to go out into the world and seek my fortune."

The king readily granted her request, bidding her to go to her step-mother, who would give her money and provisions for her journey.

"I expect you want a carriage and horses and footmen, a chest of fine robes and jewels and a basket of provisions," the step-mother said scornfully.

"Oh, no. All I want is to go as I am now and to take with me some bread and cheese and a bottle of beer," the girl answered, as this was the fare to which she had become accustomed while eating with the servants in the kitchen.

"Give the girl what she wants and let her go," the step-mother said coldly, and putting her arm round the shoulders of her own daughter, she smiled triumphantly. "Before very long the king and his people will forget all about her and you will be the only princess in Colchester, and the richest and most beautiful in the land."

Sadly the girl left the palace, and with her meagre provisions in a sack she walked through the gardens and out into the highway. After some time she turned aside, following a track which wound through lonely and deserted countryside, walking on and on until at length she realized she was quite lost.

By this time she was both hungry and tired, and so she set about looking for somewhere to rest. At last she came to a mass of fallen rocks, where a rowan tree guarded the mouth of a cave in which she decided, she could shelter for the night.

When she reached the cave, however, she found an ugly old man with a long matted beard sitting there and scowling up at her.

"What have you got in that sack?" the old man demanded.

"Stale bread, hard cheese and a bottle of beer," the girl answered.

"A meal fit for a king," the old man said. "Let us begin."

Without a word the girl sat down, opened the sack and took out the provisions which she had hoped would last her for several days. Immediately the old man began to eat ravenously, and although the girl had a mouthful of bread, a crumb of cheese and a sip of beer, he had all the rest.

"That was good," he said, when not a scrap remained, "but I noticed you have but little appetite yourself."

"Sorrow is no sauce for a meal," the girl answered with a sigh.

"A kind heart can drive away sorrow," the old man replied, and breaking a branch off the rowan tree beside them, he handed it to her.

"Keep on this path until your way is barred by a thick hedge of thorns and briars. Do not try to force your way through, but strike the hedge three times with this rowan branch and each time say 'I beg of you, hedge, of your kindness, to let me pass through'.

"When you have passed through the hedge, go on until you come to a well sheltered by a bank of yellow primroses. Look in the well and there you will see three golden heads. Whatever they ask you to do, do it willingly."

Thanking the old man for his advice, the girl set off again, and although she felt even more tired and hungry, she walked until she came to a thick hedge of thorn and briar.

Three times she struck it with her rowan branch, and three times she said,

"I beg of you, hedge, of your kindness, to let me pass through." And at the third time of asking, the hedge parted and she walked through unscratched.

On she walked until at last she came to a well sheltered by a bank of yellow primroses. Kneeling down, she looked into the water and a golden head rose from the depths, singing:

> Wash me and comb me
> And lay me down softly,
> And lay me on a bank to dry,
> That I may look pretty
> When somebody passes by.

"Certainly," said the girl, and after washing the golden head carefully, she picked up a silver comb which was lying by the edge of the well, combed the hair and laid the head gently down on the bank of yellow primroses.

Up came a second golden head, and then a third, each with the same request, and each she washed and combed and laid down gently on the bank of yellow primroses.

"How can we reward this girl who has used us so kindly?" the first golden head asked.

At last she came to a market place where everyone was busy and happy and no one had any time for her except to despise her for a moment, and she sat down by the stocks and wept bitterly.

"And what ails you?" a passing cobbler asked.

"I am the step-daughter of the King of Colchester. My face is covered with sores and my voice is like a corncrake's. I am cold and tired and no one cares what happens to me. I am more miserable than the poorest beggar in the market place." And she wept even more bitterly.

Now as it happened, the cobbler had recently mended the sandals of an old hermit, who had paid him for his kindness not with money, which he lacked, but with a jar of healing ointment and a bottle of soothing liquid of his own concoction.

"I am a kind-hearted man," said the cobbler, sitting down by the girl, "and for some time have had a mind to marry a king's daughter, provided she could cook my meals, mend my clothes and sweep out my cottage. If I heal the sores on your face with this healing ointment and restore your voice with this soothing liquid, will you marry me?"

The girl consented eagerly and she and the cobbler were married there and then.

After a few weeks the hermit's remedies worked, and it was not long before the girl began to scold and grumble in her old manner.

"I am the King of Colchester's step-daughter," she told the cobbler. "It is not fit that I should cook your meals, mend your clothes and sweep out your cottage. Let us go to the king and ask him to treat us as he treated his own daughter."

Whereupon the cobbler, who was as wise as he was kind-hearted, said nothing, but accompanied his wife back to the palace of the King of Colchester.

When the queen saw her daughter, however, and learned that she had married not a king, but a poor cobbler, she uttered a loud shriek of despair, ran out of the palace and was never seen again.

As for the king, he gave the cobbler a large sum of money on the condition that neither he nor his wife ever set foot in Colchester again.

The cobbler, having no taste for court life, was heartily glad to give his promise, and he took his wife to the farthest part of the kingdom where he lived contentedly, mending shoes, while she learned to spin and weave and generally make herself useful, but whether or not she was ever one half as happy and contented as her step-sister, I can not say.

The Red Etin

Once upon a time in the long, long ago, there lived in Scotland a poor widow with two sons. To look at, the boys were as alike as two peas, but by nature they were as different as chalk and cheese, for whereas the younger was kind and thoughtful, the other was selfish and careless.

Now the day came when the elder of the two brothers went to his mother and told her that it was high time he went out into the world to seek his fortune. Handing him a bucket, she sent him to draw water from the well so that she could bake him a bannock for his journey, but the elder brother was so absorbed by dreams of the fortune he hoped to find that he did not notice how badly the bucket was leaking nor did he hear the raven crying to him overhead. By the time he returned home the bucket was scarcely half full of water and his mother was able to bake him only a small cake of oatmeal.

"Will ye have half with my benison or the whole with my malison?" she asked.

Caring little about his mother's blessing, the elder brother said that, as he had far to journey, he would take the whole with her curse, and so concerned was he with the fortune he hoped to find that he did not notice the sadness in her eyes.

Just before he set off, he drew his brother to one side and handed him a knife.

"Look at this every morning," he said. "If the blade is bright and shining, then ye will know that all goes well with me: if, however, it is rusted and stained, then ye may be sure that some ill has befallen me and I am in sore need of help."

Off he set, and he had not travelled very far before he met an old woman who was footsore and weary.

87

"I have not eaten for many days," she said. "Can you spare me a piece of the bannock you are carrying?"

"I have not enough for myself and I certainly have not enough to give away to a beggar," the young man answered and he walked on, until, at the end of the third day, he met a man guarding a flock of sheep.

"Who owns all these sheep?" he asked, whereupon the shepherd looked up and answered:

> The Red Etin of Ireland
> Once lived in Bellygan,
> And stole King Malcolm's daughter,
> The King of fair Scotland.
> It's said there's one predestinate
> To be his mortal foe;
> But that man is yet unborn,
> And lang may it be so.

Shrugging his shoulders, the elder brother walked on and after another three days he met an old man watching over a herd of swine.

"Who owns all these swine?" he asked, whereupon the swineherd looked up and answered:

> The Red Etin of Ireland
> Once lived in Bellygan,
> And stole King Malcolm's daughter,
> The King of fair Scotland.
> It's said there's one predestinate
> To be his mortal foe;
> But that man is yet unborn,
> And lang may it be so.

Shrugging his shoulders, the elder brother walked on and after a further three days he met a very old man looking after a herd of goats.

"Who owns all these goats?" he asked, whereupon the goatherd looked up and answered:

> The Red Etin of Ireland
> Once lived in Bellygan,

And stole King Malcolm's daughter,
The King of fair Scotland.
It's said there's one predestinate
To be his mortal foe;
But that man is yet unborn,
And lang may it be so.

As the elder brother shrugged his shoulders and began to walk on, the very old goatherd shouted after him,

"Have a care of the next animals ye meet, for they are beasts of a different kind."

It was not long before the young man came face to face with a great crowd of these beasts, and when he saw that each creature had two heads and each head four horns, he was so frightened that he took to his heels and ran and ran until he came to a castle on the top of a little hill.

As the door was open, he ran straight into the kitchen, where he found an old woman dozing by the fire.

"Please let me stay here for the night," he begged. "I have journeyed far and am tired and hungry and have nowhere to go."

The old woman looked up in dismay.

"This is no place for the likes of ye. This castle belongs to the Red Etin, a cruel giant with three heads. All the ladies of high degree whom he captures are imprisoned upstairs, while as for young men like you" – she shook her head sadly – "he has never been known to spare a single one."

As the elder brother was trying to summon up enough courage to leave the castle and face the beasts of a different kind, he heard the Red Etin approaching.

"Hide me somewhere until the morning," he begged, hoping that by then the beasts would have moved away and he would be able to escape.

Hastily the old woman put him in a cupboard in a dark corner of the kitchen, and scarcely had she sat down again by the fire than the Red Etin strode in, shouting in a terrible voice:

Snouk but and snouk ben,*
I find the smell of an earthly man;

---

*"Snouk" = to smell out (Scottish). "But" = kitchen, "Ben" = living room (Scottish).

Be he living, or be he dead,
His heart this night shall kitchen my bread.

He prowled around the kitchen, sniffing suspiciously, went into the living room, where the three heads turned from side to side and the three noses sniffed again, and finally he returned to the kitchen, where his six eyes fell on the cupboard in the dark corner. Flinging open the door, he dragged out the shivering young man and shook him until his teeth rattled.

"So ye walked into the castle of the Red Etin and thought ye could hide here and then walk out again?" he roared. "Well, so ye can – if first ye can give me the answer to three questions. Which was first inhabited – Ireland or Scotland? What does man desire most in all the world? And which came first – the hen or the egg?"

When it was obvious that the young man could answer none of the questions, the giant struck him on the head with a magic hammer and turned him into a pillar of stone.

The next morning, when the younger brother looked at the knife which he had been given, he was dismayed to find it rusted and stained and he knew at once that ill fortune had befallen his brother. Not wanting to grieve his mother however, he told her that the time had come for him to go out into the world and seek his fortune.

Handing him a bucket, she sent him to draw water from the well so that she could bake him a bannock for his journey.

Just as the young man pulled up the bucket, a raven flew overhead and croaked to him to have a care and use his eyes. On seeing the water running out, the younger brother took some clay, patched up the holes, and after refilling the bucket, returned with enough water for his mother to bake him a cake more than twice as big as his brother's.

"Will ye have half with my benison or the whole with my malison?" she asked.

Because he cared a great deal for his mother, the young man chose the half with her blessing, not knowing that his half was even bigger than the whole his brother had chosen.

Away he went, walking until he was tired and hungry, and coming at last to a brown burn, he sat down, slaked his thirst and

took out his mother's bannock. Before he had enjoyed the first mouthful, an old woman hobbled up to him.

"That's a fine bannock ye've got there," she said. "Could ye spare a bite for someone who has not eaten for many a long day?"

Breaking off a piece the size of his own, he gave it to the old woman. She ate it hungrily and then stared so pointedly at the rest of the bannock that he offered her another piece and yet another, until at last she had finished it all.

"One good turn aye deserves another," she said, and she handed him a magic stick made from the wood of the rowan tree. "If ye use that rightly, it will serve ye well. Now listen carefully while I tell ye what ye must say and do, for our paths will not cross again, and if ye forget anything, ye will have the same ill fortune as your brother."

The young man listened carefully, and realizing that the old woman was one of the People of Peace, and would be angry if she were thanked, he nodded his head and set off again.

At the end of the third day he met the man guarding the flock of sheep.

"Who owns all these sheep?" he asked, whereupon the shepherd looked up and answered,

> The Red Etin of Ireland
> Once lived in Bellygan,
> And stole King Malcolm's daughter,
> The King of fair Scotland.
> But now I fear his end is near,
> And destiny at hand;
> And ye're to be, I plainly see,
> The heir of all his land.

Nodding his head, the young man walked on and after another three days he met the old man watching over the herd of swine.

"Who owns all these swine?" he asked, whereupon the swineherd looked up and answered:

> The Red Etin of Ireland
> Once lived in Bellygan,
> And stole King Malcolm's daughter,
> The King of fair Scotland.

But now I fear his end is near,
And destiny at hand;
And ye're to be, I plainly see,
The heir of all his land.

Nodding his head, the young man walked on, and after another three days he met the very old·man looking after the herd of goats.

"Who owns all these goats?" he asked, whereupon the goatherd looked up and answered:

The Red Etin of Ireland
Once lived in Bellygan,
And stole King Malcolm's daughter,
The King of fair Scotland.
But now I fear his end is near,
And destiny at hand:
And ye're to be, I plainly see,
The heir of all his land.

Nodding his head, the young man had just begun to walk on when the very old goatherd shouted after him:

"Have a care of the next animals ye meet, for they are beasts of a different kind."

It was not long before the young man came face to face with the beasts, but even when he saw that each creature had two heads and each head four horns, he was not in the least frightened. Remembering what the Woman of Peace had told him, he walked boldly on, and when one tried to attack him, he hit it with his magic stick and it ran away, bellowing loudly.

On the young man walked until at last he came to the castle on the top of the hill, and as the door was open, he went straight into the kitchen, where he found an old woman dozing by the fire.

"Please let me stay here for the night," he said. "I am tired and hungry and have nowhere to go."

The old woman looked up in dismay.

"This is no place for the likes of ye. This castle belongs to the Red Etin, a cruel giant with three heads. All the ladies of high degree whom he captures are imprisoned upstairs, while as for the last young man – who looked exactly like ye do – I dare not tell ye his fate."

Nothing that the old woman said could frighten the young man or persuade him to leave the castle, but at last, on hearing the giant approach, he allowed himself to be hidden in a cupboard in a dark corner of the kitchen.

As soon as the giant came in, he shouted out in a terrible voice:

> Snouk but and snouk ben,
> I find the smell of an earthly man;
> Be he living or be he dead.
> His heart this night shall kitchen my bread.

He prowled around the kitchen, sniffing suspiciously, went into the living room where the three heads turned from side to side and the three noses sniffed again, and finally he returned to the kitchen to find the young man now sitting by the fire, opposite the old woman, and not in the least afraid.

"So ye walked into the castle of the Red Etin and thought ye could sit by my fire and then walk out again?" he roared. "Well so ye can – if first ye can give me the answer to three questions. Which was first inhabited – Ireland or Scotland? What does man desire most in all the world? And which came first – the hen or the egg?"

As the Woman of Peace had foretold all that would happen, the young man was able to give the correct answers and the Red Etin immediately lost all his magic powers.

"The world has had enough of ye," the young man said, and seizing the giant's own axe, he cut off the three heads with a single stroke. And that was the end of the Red Etin.

Taking the keys which hung from the giant's belt, the young man climbed up the stairs and unlocked all the doors, setting free the beautiful ladies who had been imprisoned in the castle, but when he opened the last door he bowed very low, because this lady was more beautiful than any of the others and he knew at once that she must be King Malcolm's daughter, the King of fair Scotland.

The young man returned with the ladies to the kitchen, where the old woman still sat by the fire.

"I have opened every room in the castle and nowhere is there any sign of my brother," he said. "Do you know where he is?"

"Follow me," the old woman answered, and led him down to a dark cellar in the middle of which stood a stone pillar. Stepping forward the young man touched the pillar with his magic stick and immediately his elder brother stood before him, well and strong.

Everyone rejoiced that the wicked Red Etin was no more, and the two brothers set off with the princess and the other ladies, to make sure that they reached safely the court of King Malcolm, the King of fair Scotland.

When the king heard all that had happened, he was so pleased that he gave his consent to the marriage of his daughter and the young man who had rescued her. He found a rich and beautiful wife for the elder brother and gave orders that their widowed mother should be provided for, and they all lived happily for the rest of their days.

Wee Robin Redbreast

Once upon a winter's morning, wee Robin Redbreast was sitting on his own special branch of a briar bush which stretched out over the chuckling waters of a burn somewhere in the Lowlands of Scotland.

So happy was he and so merrily did he sing that all the other birds in the trees and bushes nearby and in the sky above fell silent, the better to listen to him.

"There is no doubt about it," a mistle-thrush said, in his harsh grating voice, "Wee Robin Redbreast is the finest singer in the whole of Scotland."

"No doubt at all," the other birds agreed.

"What a pity it is," the mistle-thrush continued, "that the king and queen on their golden thrones, and all the courtiers dressed in velvet and their ladies dressed in silk, can not hear wee Robin sing on this fine winter's morning."

"And why should he not fly off and sing to them?" the owl asked, opening one eye and then falling asleep again.

"Why not, indeed!" wee Robin answered. "I shall practise once more and then I'll be off."

Opening wide his beak, he sang higher and clearer than ever before, with many a sweet note and many a deft twitter.

Just as he finished and was spreading his wings to fly south, who should come along, velvet-footed, but the old grey farm cat: stopping by the briar bush, she licked her lips with her pink tongue and gazed up at wee Robin with a sly expression.

"Good day to you, wee Robin," she said softly. "And where are you off to this fine winter's morning?"

"I'm off to see the king and the queen on their golden thrones,

96

and all the courtiers dressed in velvet and their ladies dressed in silk, and I'm going to sing my winter song to them," wee Robin answered.

"What a fine idea," the sly puss said. "But before you go, why not fly down to the ground here and let me show you the pretty white ribbon round my neck?"

"Oh, no, sly Puss. No, no, no! You may be cunning enough to catch a wee mouse, but you're not cunning enough to catch me," and away he flew through the frosty air until at length he came to a sheepfold. There he saw, perched on the wall, a greedy kite, cruel eyes gleaming in his pale head.

"Good day to you, wee Robin," the kite said smoothly. "And where are you off to this fine winter's morning?"

"I'm off to see the king and queen on their golden thrones, and all the courtiers dressed in velvet and their ladies dressed in silk, and I'm going to sing my winter's song to them," wee Robin answered.

"What a fine idea," the greedy kite said. "But before you go, why not fly across here and I'll show you the white blaze on my wing feathers?"

"Oh, no, greedy Kite. No, no, no! You've swooped down on the wee linnets and made a meal of them, but you'll not make a meal of me," and away he flew through the frosty air until at length he came to a high crag. At the foot of the crag there was a cave where lay a crafty fox.

"Good day to you, wee Robin," the fox said with a false smile. "And where are you off to this fine winter's morning?"

"I'm off to see the king and queen on their golden thrones, and all the courtiers dressed in velvet and their ladies dressed in silk, and I'm going to sing my winter's song to them," wee Robin answered.

"What a fine idea," the crafty old fox said. "But before you go, why not just fly down here and I'll show you the pretty spot on the end of my tail?"

"Oh, no, crafty old Fox. No, no, no! You've jumped out on the poor wee lambs and eaten them, but you'll not eat me," and away he flew through the frosty air until at length he came to the bank of a wide river, and there a young lad was sitting, kicking his heels idly.

"Good day to you, Robin," the idle lad cried with a knowing smile. "And where are you off to this fine winter's morning?"

"I'm off to see the king and queen on their golden thrones, and all the courtiers dressed in velvet and their ladies dressed in silk, and I'm going to sing my winter's song to them."

"What a fine idea," the idle lad cried. "But before you go, why not just fly across here and I'll give you a handful of oats from my pocket?"

"Oh, no, idle Lad. No, no, no! You've snared the trusting goldfinch that way, but you'll not snare me," and away he flew through the frosty air, and on and on and on he flew, until at last he came to a splendid palace.

Round and round he flew until he found the great hall, and there he saw the king and queen sitting on their golden thrones at the top of a long table; along one side were the courtiers dressed in velvet and along the other their ladies dressed in silk, and they were all feasting and enjoying themselves.

Down to the window sill flew wee Robin and opened his beak and sang his winter song, even higher and clearer than when he had sung it on the briar bush, and with notes so sweet and twitters so deft that the courtiers exclaimed in amazement, and the ladies clapped their hands and begged for more. As for the king and queen, they declared that never in their lives had they heard such a fine winter song.

When the Robin had finished singing a second time, the king turned to the queen.

"That was just fine," he cried.

"Indeed it was," she agreed.

"And what can we give wee Robin Redbreast for singing us this winter song?" he asked.

"What about giving him a wee wren to be his wife?" the queen suggested.

And that is exactly what they did.

Wee Robin and wee Wren were married that very same day in the hall of the splendid palace, and the king and queen and all the courtiers in velvet and their ladies in silk danced at the wedding; and then wee Robin flew back with his wife to the Lowlands of Scotland and the briar bush which grew by the chuckling waters of the burn, and there they lived together happily ever after.

King Arthur and the Shepherd Laddie

Many years ago a young shepherd laddie lived with his father and mother and little sister in a humble cottage near the ruins of a castle in the far north of England.

He had never been to school, because in that part of the country there was no school to go to, and in any case, shepherd laddies and lasses had to work almost as soon as they could walk and so had no time for lessons.

He could neither read nor write, but he had a pair of keen eyes which missed nothing that went on around him, and a pair of sharp ears which heard all that he was meant to hear – and quite a lot that he wasn't.

At times he could be careless and forgetful, but because he was always so willing and cheerful and whistled and sang from morning till night, his parents loved him dearly and his little sister thought there was no one else like him in the whole world.

In the summer he would sit on the great stone wall which crowned Sewingshields Crags and ran along the high, rocky cliff to east and west as far as the eye could see. From there he could keep watch on the black-faced sheep that cropped the grass in the broad ditch and sloping banks surrounding the ruined castle below, and he could look far north over the bogs and wasteland in case a thief might take it into his mind to help himself to any of his flock.

Sometimes the laddie would take his little sister with him for company and they would sit side by side on the wall above the Crags, and to the busy click-click of their knitting needles – because everyone, men, women and children, knitted in those days – they would keep an eye on the sheep while they chattered of all that had happened down in the master's farm and in the neighbouring cottages.

"Some people say that this wall on which we are now sitting was built by the giants," the little lass said to her brother one day as the wind was sending the clouds scudding across the sky.

"That's what I thought when I was young," her brother answered, in a very grown-up manner. "But only last week I heard the master talking to a friend, and he said that he had just been entertaining a gentleman who was travelling in his own coach and with his own servants, and this gentleman said the wall was built by the Romans and stretched right across the country from the North Sea to the Solway Firth. But who the Romans were, I don't know. And I don't know where the Solway Firth is, either. But I shall find out one day."

"Do you think the Romans had anything to do with King Arthur and his queen and the Knights of the Round Table?" the lass asked, remembering the stories their mother used to tell them in the dark winter evenings as they huddled around the fire.

"I don't think so," her brother answered, and both children looked down from the wall and past their cottage to the ruins of Sewingshields Castle where – so their mother said – King Arthur and his court had once lived in great splendour.

"That reminds me," the little lass cried suddenly, "that when I was helping to churn the butter yesterday, the packman came by with his wares. Oh, the lovely ribbons and laces he had, the rolls of cloth and the shiny pins and needles! And the dairymaid asked him in and gave him some milk to drink, and he told us all about the places he'd visited, and who was engaged and who was married, and who had new babies and who had died.

"Then he said he'd come all the way from London, where he'd seen the queen, sitting on her golden throne.

"Of course we laughed, and the dairymaid said that she dared say the next place he went to he'd be telling them he'd seen King Arthur asleep in his cave in Sewingshields Crags, with his queen beside him and his knights and hounds around him.

"Just imagine – he didn't know anything at all about them. King Arthur asleep here all these hundreds of years and he didn't even know."

"Did you tell him about the treasure that was waiting for the first person who found the cave and wakened the king?" the laddie asked.

"I didn't, but the dairymaid did. He got quite excited and said he was off to find the cave straight away. I said he'd better wait and hear about the spell and how to break it, but he said he didn't believe in spells and all he wanted was the treasure."

"That's just silly," her brother said, frowning. "Everyone says the spell is the most important part of all." He stopped knitting. "Did you tell him how to break it?"

The lass's face crimsoned and her fingers flew faster than ever.

"I couldn't remember it properly. I know there's a table with a bugle and a sword and a garter on it, but I just couldn't remember just what you have to do with them."

"All right. There's no need to worry. It's probably as well that you couldn't. We don't want every wandering packman hunting for our king and our treasure, do we?"

"No, we don't," the lass agreed and they both continued knitting contentedly.

Day after day the shepherd laddie watched his master's sheep, knitted his stockings – and thought about the conversation he'd had with his sister.

At first he was inclined to feel sorry for King Arthur, sleeping for hundreds and hundreds of years. Surely he would be glad to be awakened, especially on a fine summer's day such as this one, when the sun was high in the sky and the lark was singing so sweetly, and down in the castle ditch the butterflies were flitting round the meadowsweet and enchanter's nightshade.

And then he thought about the treasure and how wonderful it would be to be rich.

The treasure! That settled it. He hadn't very much spare time, but what he had, he decided, would be spent from now on looking for King Arthur's cave in Sewingshields Crags.

It wasn't long before his father realized what he was doing.

"You're wasting your time, laddie," he said. "Better men than you have looked for that cave and haven't found it. Why don't you do something useful like feeding the hens and digging the vegetable patch?"

The laddie fed the hens and dug the vegetable patch and then, without a word to anyone, continued his search.

By the time autumn came he had found several caves, but the only inhabitants were foxes who were not asleep and who did not like being disturbed.

Colder grew the winds as winter settled in and presently the ground was covered with snow and the little lakes to the north-west of the Crags were frozen over. Now, if the laddie had any time to think of King Arthur, it was to envy him the warmth and comfort of his cave, to wish that he too could drowse by the fire instead of going out to feed his master's stock, his fingers and toes so chilled with the cold that they lost all feeling.

With the return of spring and the busy lambing season, he soon forgot about winter's trials. He would probably have forgotten all about King Arthur too – or, at any rate, have decided there were better ways of passing what little leisure time he had than in hunting for his cave – had it not been for his carelessness one blustery day in May.

He was sitting, as usual, on the top of the wall on Sewingshields Crags knitting another pair of socks for the following winter, when a rather too quick tug sent the precious ball of wool rolling away from him, over the cliff edge, unwinding down the steep rock face, to disappear finally among the tumbled rocks below.

As the cliff was much too dangerous to climb down from the place where he had been sitting, he glanced around quickly to make sure that all his lambs and ewes were safe, that there was no fox in sight on the ground, no bird of prey in the air, and then he hurried off, leaving his knitting and needles held firmly in place by a large stone.

Along the wall he hurried to where it dipped to a narrow pass and, once through the farm gate, he ran back along the green field where his flock was grazing.

He could see the thick, grey wool stretching down from the top of the Crags to the fallen rocks which each winter's storms dislodged. Clambering between clumps of stinging nettles, thorny briars and sharp-needled whins, at last he reached the line of wool, but the ball itself was nowhere to be seen.

It had disappeared in a cranny between two large grey boulders.

Pushing and heaving at the nearer of these, he managed to move it enough to make out his ball of wool lying in the gloom, just out of reach of his straining fingers.

Again he pushed and heaved, until at length he managed to move the boulder sufficiently to allow him to edge in sideways and pick up his precious ball.

As he was about to work his way back, he suddenly realized that it was not a cranny into which his ball had fallen, but the entrance to a low passage, and that far away in the heart of the rock a strange green light flickered.

I've found it, he thought, his heart beating wildly with excitement. I've found the entrance to the cave where King Arthur sleeps, with his queen beside him and all his knights and his hounds. When I waken the king he will give me a great treasure as a reward and I'll give all of it – well, most of it – to my father. We'll have sheep and beasts of our own so that we won't have to work for the master from dawn to sunset and we'll have warm clothes to wear in winter so that we're never cold again, and so much food to eat that we'll never be hungry either.

Bending almost double, he crept along the low passage, his excitement ebbing a little as he left behind the comforting sunshine, and the strange green light closed around him.

Slower and slower he walked, his back aching because he had to crouch so low to avoid hitting his head against the roof.

Sleeping lizards opened heavy eyes and glared balefully at him. Huge toads croaked harshly at this creature who dared to disturb their age-long peace. Sticky cobwebs clung to his face and hands as he crept along and black bats, hanging from the roof, rustled dryly as he brushed against them, and then unfolded their wings to swoop menacingly around him, as though trying to prevent his going on any further.

He was frightened.

He had never been so frightened in all his life.

But the thought of the treasure, of having enough to eat and wear for the rest of his life, gave him the courage to stumble on.

Now the green light was growing brighter and the passage broader and higher so that there was no need to stoop – and suddenly he found himself at the entrance to a great vaulted hall, bigger even than the priory church at Hexham, where his uncle had taken him one Christmas Eve.

In the centre of the hall burned the magic green fire which grew bright and then dimmed as the flames rose and sank, but what fed that fire he didn't know, for there was neither wood nor peat nor coal to replenish it.

Round the fire a pack of splendid hounds slumbered, eyes closed, flanks rising and falling as they breathed slowly and evenly.

On couches beside the tapestry-hung walls slept knights in armour and ladies in splendid silken gowns, while at the far end of the hall, on thrones of gold and wearing golden crowns and velvet robes trimmed with fur, sat the great King, Arthur, and his Queen, Guinevere, both peacefully sleeping. Beside the king's throne stood a carved wooden chest, its lid thrown back to reveal a pile of emeralds and diamonds, pearls and amethysts, rubies and topazes and all manner of precious stones, which winked and gleamed and shone in the magic light.

Fearfully the laddie advanced into the hall. His foot brushed against a sleeping hound and he jumped back in alarm, but the beast never stirred and there was no change at all in its even breathing.

As he drew nearer to the sleeping king, he now saw the lines of weariness and sorrow on the still face, and he recalled the stories his mother had told him – of those who had tried to take Arthur's kingdom from him, of that last great fight when, badly wounded, he was taken by the three queens to be cared for at Avalon and was then brought by Merlin to rest here, secure in the heart of Sewingshields Crags.

Now his gaze fell on the oak table in front of the throne and he stared, fascinated, at the great sword in its engraved scabbard, the silver mounted hunting horn and the silken garter which lay beside them.

Whoever found the king had to perform three tasks to break the spell, he thought, and once the spell was broken and the king awake, the treasure would be his.

But were the tasks really necessary after all? The king looked so tired that perhaps he wouldn't want to be wakened just yet.

The laddie hesitated. Why not help himself? Not too many of the gleaming jewels. Just a handful. Enough to buy food and clothes for many years.

Approaching the chest boldly he bent down, one hand outstretched – and then he jumped back with a loud cry of alarm.

No one moved. Nothing stirred. But it was just as though a thousand nettles had stung his hand.

Frightened, he examined it, but there was nothing to see – no swelling, no angry red marks. Even when the sharp stinging began to die away, so terrifying was the memory that he dared not reach out a second time. The jewels, he knew now, were protected by the spell and that had first to be broken.

He approached the table and, very slowly, reached out his hand and touched the sword hilt, afraid that he might feel the sharp stinging pain again.

Nothing happened.

Growing more confident, he grasped the hilt firmly in his right hand, held the beautiful engraved scabbard in his left, and drew out the shining blade.

The rhythm of the sleepers' breathing altered and the laddie looked up quickly to see the faint flutter of the queen's eyelashes, and the king's eyes open slowly, while on their couches the knights and ladies sighed and murmured softly.

Trembling at the thought that, of all the people in Northumberland, it was he who had been chosen to break the powerful spell, the laddie tightened his grip on the hilt, lifted the silken garter from the table, and with the same steady stroke he used when chopping wood, he cut the garter in two, so that one half dropped back on the table and the other remained in his hand.

Round the fire the hounds grunted, snuffled, shook themselves, and, very unsteadily, got to their feet. There was the soft whisper of silken robes and the clang of armour as queen and king, ladies and knights stretched their arms and flexed first one leg and then the other.

He had done it, the laddie rejoiced. He had broken the spell and fame and fortune were his. The excitement went to his head, making him careless and forgetful.

Eyes gleaming, he slipped the point of the sword back into the scabbard and slid the blade down, but just as the hilt came to rest against the scabbard, a great moaning sigh filled the hall and the green flame shot up until it licked the fretted beams of the ceiling.

Still seated on his golden throne, King Arthur raised his hands, stared at the now trembling laddie with cold, grey eyes, and cried out in a terrible voice:

> O, woe betide that evil day
> On which this witless wight was born,
> Who drew the sword, the garter cut,
> But never blew the bugle horn.

His voice echoed and re-echoed in the vast hall, and the sighs of the queen and knights and ladies washed over the laddie as, unable to move from the spot, he saw the eyelids flutter and close, the limbs come to rest until everyone – king, queen, knights, ladies and hounds – was plunged in the same profound, enchanted sleep in which he had first found them.

Down sank the green flame, dwindling, dying, robbing the hall and the sleepers of all colour, while the laddie stood there, sick with disappointment and terrified that he too had fallen a victim to the spell, and was doomed to spend the rest of his life in the cave under the Crags.

At last, just before the flame finally expired, he made a great effort, moved first one hand and then the other, first one foot and then the other, and finding his limbs obeyed him, turned and ran out of the hall, blundering along the passage where the bats and toads and lizards protested at this second intrusion, until at last he wriggled out into the sunshine and without even stopping to draw his breath, made for his home as fast as ever he could.

When his father heard what had happened, he shook his head sadly.

"Of all the times to be forgetful and careless," he said, "you had to choose this afternoon. Take me to the entrance before anyone else hears about it and I'll break the spell properly. I'll not forget to blow the bugle horn. The king was right. You certainly didn't have your wits about you today."

But when the laddie returned with his father to the foot of the Crags, the wind had snapped the dangling line of wool, the ball was nowhere to be seen and neither was the entrance to the cave. All evening they searched, and the following day too. But they searched in vain.

As soon as the farmers and labourers living nearby heard the amazing tale, they too joined in the hunt, all eager to break the spell, awaken King Arthur and win for themselves a great treasure.

But no one ever found the entrance again.

At first the laddie was inconsolable, and his mother and little sister were very distressed because he had no appetite and no longer laughed and sang as he used to do.

Until one day, when the dairymaid remembered something she had heard and told the lass, who immediately hurried up to the wall on top of Sewingshields Crags where her brother was sitting, sadly watching the sheep.

"It seems to me it's a very good thing you didn't break the spell," she cried. "The dairymaid says that when Merlin cast his spell on King Arthur and all his knights, he declared it was only to be broken when the country was in danger and needed them to come to the rescue."

"Oh!" the laddie said thoughtfully.

"We don't need them now," the lass continued. "Everyone is very happy and peaceful and the Border raiders no longer ride down from Liddesdale and Tynedale, from Gilsland and Bewcastle, as they did in our grandfather's day, to steal the sheep and cattle and set fire to the homesteads."

"That's quite true," her brother agreed.

"What would you have said if you had wakened the king and he'd asked you who it was he had to fight? I don't think he'd have been very pleased when you said he wasn't needed at all, and I don't think he'd have rewarded you with any treasure."

"You're quite right," the laddie answered, beginning to cheer up immediately.

His little sister smiled, because she loved her brother dearly and hated to see him looking unhappy.

His mother smiled, because she was sure they could manage very well as they were.

As for his father, he was most relieved, because he knew that if his son had brought home a treasure, it would have attracted to Sewingshields all the thieves and cut-throats, and he and his family would have lived in fear for the rest of their lives.

So it is that, because the shepherd laddie forgot how to break Merlin's spell, King Arthur, his queen, and all his knights and ladies and hounds still slumber in the cave beneath Sewingshields Crags, waiting, not just for someone to draw the sword, cut the garter and blow the horn, but for the day when England is in real danger and needs its heroes of old to come to her rescue.

True Thomas

One fine summer's day, more than seven hundred years ago, True Thomas – whom many called Thomas the Rhymer – was wandering along the banks of the Leader Water which flows through the Lauderdale valley, in the Scottish Borderland. To the splashing of the burn was added the hum of bees as they sought their honey from white eyebright, sweet-smelling thyme, blue veronica and the golden flowers of lady's bedstraw, while high above a lark sang passionately in the cloudless sky.

When True Thomas came to the Eildon Tree on Huntlie Bank, he lay down and stretched himself out in its shade. Breathing deeply of the sweet-scented air, he tried to make, from all the sounds and colours around him, a perfect poem accompanied by perfect music – such a poem as he could sing to his friends some evening in his home, the Tower of Ercildoune.

But words do not always come when poets most desire them, and although he closed his eyes the better to concentrate, now those sights and sounds which had first seemed to inspire him began to fill him with despair that they should succeed in creating perfect beauty and music while he failed so completely.

Just when he was convinced that never again would he put words together to make a poem, or notes to make music, he heard a new sound – softer, sweeter and more enchanting than any he had ever heard before in all the brave Borderland.

Opening his eyes, he stared, incredulous, at the fair lady who was riding towards him from the slopes of the Eildon Hills, where often he had walked and hunted.

Over a gown of grass-green silk she wore a cloak of the finest velvet, and the mane of her milk-white steed was plaited and hung with nine and fifty bells, bells whose music was softer, sweeter and more enchanting than anything True Thomas had ever heard.

So fair was the lady, so splendid her steed, so enchanting the music of the silver bells, that the poet did not know whether he was awake or dreaming, and it was not until the lady reined her horse beside the Eildon Tree that he realized this was neither dream nor imagination, and springing to his feet, he pulled off his velvet cap and bowed low before such loveliness.

"Ye must be the Queen of Heaven herself," he whispered, "for never in all my life have I seen a lady as fair as ye."

Looking down on the handsome young man kneeling before her, the lady smiled.

"Ye are mistaken, True Thomas. I am indeed a queen, but the country I rule is fair Elfland and I have journeyed from there today because of ye, Thomas."

Slipping down from the back of her steed, she stood in front of the poet and looked up into his eyes, and at that moment True Thomas knew that he had lost his heart forever.

"How brave a man are ye, True Thomas? Brave enough to kiss my lips, knowing that afterwards ye will be mine, whether it be for weal or woe?"

"I am as brave as any man," True Thomas answered. "Whether it be for good or ill, I am not afraid of ye," and taking the fair queen in his arms, he kissed her on the lips, under the Eildon Tree, and the lark sang a sweeter song than he had ever heard it sing before.

"I warned ye, True Thomas," the queen said softly. "Now ye must leave Ercildoune and all the brave Borderland: now ye must go with me to fair Elfland and serve me faithfully, whether it be for weal or for woe, for full seven years."

"I am well content that it should be so," True Thomas answered.

Lightly the queen mounted her milk-white steed, and lightly True Thomas sprang up behind her, underneath the Eildon Tree. On the bridle and on the plaited mane the silver bells rang sweetly as away they sped, faster than the wind, on and on and ever faster and still yet faster.

They left behind the brave Borderland with its hills and burns,

its heather and bracken and green, green grass and its many-coloured flowers, and at length they came to a flat, mysterious country which True Thomas had never seen before, and there the queen reined her steed and both dismounted.

Spreading out her skirts of grass-green silk, she sat down and beckoned to True Thomas, and when he had seated himself beside her, she cradled his head in her lap.

"Now we must rest a while and talk a while," she said, "because now we have come to the very end of your world and I have something to show you which is both strange and wonderful," and lifting up one fair hand, she pointed straight ahead.

"O see ye not yon narrow road
So thick beset with thorns and briars?
That is the path of righteousness,
Though after it but few enquires."

"I see yon narrow road," answered True Thomas, "and because I know the world and the men and women who live in it, I can well believe that few enquire after the road of righteousness." And he sighed that this should be so.

"And see not ye that braid, braid road,
That lies across the lily leven?
That is the path of wickedness,
Though some call it the road to heaven."

"I see that broad, broad road which is the path of wickedness," answered True Thomas, "and because I know the world and the men and women who live in it, I can well believe that many call it the road to heaven." And he sighed again that this should be so.

"And see not ye that bonny road
That winds about the fernie brae?
That is the road to fair Elfland,
Where thou and I this night maun gae."

"I see the bonny road that winds about the hillside," answered True Thomas, "and I am content, and more than content to follow it with ye to fair Elfland." And now he had done with sighing and would have sprung to his feet had not the queen restrained him with a hand on his shoulder.

"There is one other matter that ye must know, True Thomas. During the seven years that ye dwell in fair Elfland, do not speak a single word or ye will never return to Ercildoune on the Leader Water, and the Borderland ye love so well."

And True Thomas, because he loved his own country so well, promised that never a word would he speak in fair Elfland.

Again the queen mounted her milk-white steed and True Thomas sprang up behind her, and on they rode, swifter than the wind, league after weary league. True Thomas knew neither where they were nor in which direction they were going, as the darkness pressed in on them on all sides, and there was neither sun nor moon to light their way, and the only sound was the crash and roar of breakers on an unseen sea.

Denser and more frightening grew the darkness as they rode through rivers which reached to their knees, and fear gripped True Thomas because, although he could see nothing, he knew these were no chattering burns they were crossing.

"Trust me, True Thomas," the queen said. "In your world there are always wars and bloodshed, and all the blood shed there runs through the rivers of this country."

Just when it seemed he could endure the journey no longer, the roar of the angry seas died away, the darkness lifted and True Thomas saw that now they were in a garden more beautiful than any he had seen on earth, a garden where trees bore fruit and flowers at the same time: the song of the birds was sweeter even than that of the lark which had sung high above the Eildon Tree, and among the green grass bloomed flowers more wondrous than white eyebright, sweet-smelling thyme, veronica and golden lady's bedstraw.

"At last I am come to fair Elfland," he said, and he was well content.

For a little space the queen looked at the handsome poet, and then, turning, she plucked an apple from the nearest tree.

> "Take this for thy wages, True Thomas;
> It will give thee the tongue that can never lee."

True Thomas stared at the queen in dismay.

"What kind of a gift is it that ye have given me, to tell me that my tongue will always speak the truth? Ye must know little of the ways of my world, fair queen, or of the men and women who dwell in it.

"How could I go to the Border fairs and markets, and bargain with farmers and traders who wanted to buy something from me or sell something to me, if all I could speak was the truth? When I went to court – as sometimes I do – I dared not open my mouth if I knew I had to say what I really thought. And how could I talk to a lady and flatter her – and all ladies expect to be flattered as ye yourself must know, fair queen – if all I could speak was the truth?"

The queen laughed at his dismay.

"It is no use railing against fate, True Thomas. The gift is yours whether ye like it or not. But be comforted. It will serve ye better than ye think. When ye return to your own brave Borderland, ye will have the gift of seeing into the future, and your tongue will speak of marvels yet undreamed of, and of wonders that are to come to fair Scotland long after ye and those who know ye have gone.

"But now ye must forget about your own country and enjoy yourself in fair Elfland. Because ye are bound to serve me for seven years, I promise ye that, never shall ye rue the day ye kissed me under the Eildon Tree."

She had new clothes made for him – green velvet shoes, fine, hose and a rich doublet trimmed with fur – so that he looked more handsome than ever, and for seven magic years True Thomas forgot about the Borderland and the Eildon Tree by the Leader Water, and he dwelt with the queen, and in all that time he knew neither sorrow nor care.

On the very last night of the seven years, he fell asleep on his silken couch in Elfland, but when he opened his eyes the next morning, he found himself lying on Huntlie Bank, under the Eildon Tree, and the grass was sprinkled with white eyebright, sweet-smelling thyme, veronica and the golden flowers of lady's bedstraw, while high above, a lark sang passionately in the cloudless sky.

Was it all a dream, he wondered, as slowly, sadly, he rose to his feet and stared about him, but when he went back to Ercildoune, his neighbours and friends were astonished and delighted.

"Where have ye been, True Thomas?" they cried. "For seven

long years we have not seen ye, and those that loved ye feared ye were dead and mourned for ye. Have ye been journeying in foreign lands and fighting against the pagan enemy? Tell us where ye have been and all ye have done and seen."

"I have been – dreaming," True Thomas answered, and he returned to his Tower of Ercildoune. There he made his poems and looked into the future, and told people of marvels yet undreamed of and of the wonders that were to come to Scotland long after he and they had gone.

His prophecies were written down by many of the men who heard them, prophecies which foretold the sudden death of kings hundreds of years later and the fate of great houses and noble families in this present century, and everything True Thomas said happened as he foretold, because he had been given the gift by the Queen of fair Elfland.

But if True Thomas forgot about Ercildoune on the Leader Water when he was in Elfland, he never forgot about that magic country when he returned to the Borderland, and many a time when his friends were talking and laughing, one of them would hear him sigh softly, and turning, would see a faraway look in his eye.

True Thomas loved the Borderland with its hills and burns, its heather and bracken: he loved too the beautiful ladies who visited him and flattered him and listened so eagerly to his poems and songs, and he enjoyed the company of the men with whom he went hunting by day and talked and feasted long into the night – but always there remained with him the memory of Elfland and the fair queen he loved more than life itself. Some day she will send a sign for me and I shall know the time has come for me to return to her forever, he thought, but what the sign would be or when the day would come, he knew not.

The years passed pleasantly and True Thomas's fame as a poet and seer spread throughout Scotland, and many famous men and women came to visit and consult him in his Tower of Ercildoune, and he welcomed them all and offered them shelter and hospitality.

It was on one such occasion, when both friends and strangers were gathered round the table in the Tower, talking and feasting, that a little page ran into the hall, so excited that scarce could he find the words he wanted.

"A hart!" he cried at last. "A hart and a hind too. The woodcutter saw them come out of the forest and now they are walking down the village street. A hart and a hind, both milk-white. And no man dare lift his hand against them."

Silence fell on the company, for everyone knew these were no earthly creatures.

With a smile True Thomas rose to his feet, aware that this was the sign he had been waiting for and that at last the time had come to return to the queen he loved and to fair Elfland.

Out into the street he walked where the two noble beasts awaited him and then they turned, and with True Thomas following a pace behind, they led the way back up the street, and the guests, peering in wonder and amazement from the door of the tower, watched in silence as the three forms vanished into the dark shadows of the forest and were never seen on earth again.

It is over seven hundred years since True Thomas – whom some call Thomas the Rhymer – lived in the Scottish Borderland. Ercildoune is now called Earlston, and nearby are ivy-covered ruins which are still called the Rhymer's Tower. The Eildon Tree, which once stood on Huntlie Bank on the eastern slopes of the Eildon Hills, has long since died, but in its place there is a big stone to mark for all time the place where True Thomas first met the Queen of Elfland and loved her more than life itself.

"We can give her a fairer fortune than she has known recently," the second head answered.

"Yes, that is what we must do," the third head agreed.

"Her voice shall be sweeter than the sound of silver bells," the first head said.

"She shall be even more beautiful than she is now," said the second head.

"She shall marry the most handsome king in the land, who will love her dearly because she is good and kind," added the third head.

"Thank you kindly," the girl said.

"Now place us back in the well and leave the silver comb where you found it," the three heads ordered, and the girl did as she was bid and set off on her travels again, even more tired and hungry than before.

Presently she heard the cry of hounds and the thud of horses' hoofs, and seeing a hunt approaching, she drew in to one side, hoping none of the fine lords would notice her.

But the leading huntsman — who was a king and more handsome than any who followed him — caught sight of her and immediately forgetting about the chase, reined his horse, dismounted, and went over to her.

For a long time he stared at her without speaking, and finally he declared that she was so beautiful that he had fallen in love with her and would not know a moment's happiness until she had promised to marry him. When she tried to reason with him, her voice was sweeter than the sound of silver bells, so that he fell even deeper in love, and he begged her to return with him to his palace, where he might convince her of his affection.

After some time the girl decided she had come to love the king as much as he loved her, and they were married amidst great rejoicings. When the wedding feast was over, they set off in a coach drawn by six magnificent horses and followed by the most handsome of the courtiers and the most beautiful of the ladies-in-waiting, to visit the King of Colchester.

The moment the king saw his daughter again he remembered how good and kind she had always been. He could see, too, how beautiful she was, and when he learned that she was married to the greatest and most handsome king in all the land, he was very

The Three Golden Heads

sorry for the way he had treated her and immediately he gave orders for a splendid banquet to be prepared in honour of his daughter and her husband.

Everyone in Colchester rejoiced at the good news – everyone except the ugly stepmother and her ugly daughter.

All day and every day the daughter grumbled about her step-sister's good fortune in marrying such a handsome and wealthy king, until at last her mother lost her temper and boxed her ears.

"If you are not satisfied in Colchester," she said, "do as your step-sister did. Go out into the world and seek your fortune."

Putting on her richest gown, the daughter summoned her carriage and horses and footmen; inside the carriage she ordered the servants to place one chest of fine clothes, another of jewels and a basket filled with roast pigeons, lemon pies, pancakes, brandy snaps, a large seed cake and a bottle of wine.

Off she drove, through the garden and along the highway, but before very long the horses went lame, the footmen – who disliked her heartily – ran back to the palace, thieves stole the chests of robes and jewels and the girl only just succeeded in escaping up a track with the basket containing her provisions.

Grumbling to herself all the time, she walked on and on, until at last she came to the mass of fallen rock where the rowan tree guarded a cave and here, she decided, she would shelter for the night.

When she reached the mouth of the cave, however, she found an ugly old man with a long matted beard sitting and scowling up at her.

"What have you got in that basket?" the old man demanded.

"Mind your own business," the daughter retorted, as she took out the roast pigeons, lemon pies, pancakes, brandy snaps, the large seed cake and the bottle of wine.

"A meal fit for a king," the old man said. "Let us begin."

He stretched out his hand but the daughter knocked it away and boxed his ears for good measure, and then she began to eat ravenously until there was not a crumb left and the wine bottle was empty.

"What about me?" the old man asked.

"Pick yourself some berries from the hedges. Hunger is a fine sauce for a meal."

The Three Golden Heads

"May bad fortune follow you," the old man cried angrily, but the girl only laughed and, much refreshed, walked on until s... came to a thick hedge of thorn and briar.

Without stopping to think, she tried to force her way throug... but the thorns scratched her hands and face and the briars tore... shreds her rich gown so that she was weeping with pain and ang... when finally she reached the other side.

On she walked again until at last she came to a well of clea... water, sheltered by a bank of yellow primroses.

Kneeling down to gaze at her reflection, she was surprised... see a golden head rise from the depths, singing:

Wash me and comb me
And lay me down softly,
And lay me on a bank to dry,
That I may look pretty
When somebody passes by.

"Wash you and comb you? Certainly not," the daughter crie... and she pushed the head back into the depths of the well. Sh... treated the second and third golden heads in the same manne... picked up the silver comb and put it in her pocket for her own us... and was just about to go away when the three heads rose to t... surface again.

"How can we reward this girl who has used us so unkindly?... the first head asked.

"We can give her the kind of fortune she deserves," the secon... head answered.

"Yes, that is what we can do," the third agreed.

"Let her face be covered with sores," the first head said.

"Let her voice be as harsh as a corncrake's," said the second head.

"She shall marry the poorest man in the land, who will treat her as she deserves to be treated," added the third head.

Bad-tempered and frightened, the girl ran off and back to the highway, but whenever she spoke to passing travellers, they laughed at her, and whenever she looked at them, they turned away in disgust, so that at last she knew that what the heads in the well had foretold had indeed come true.

R